The Cartographer of Forgotten Fronts (Book I)

Frank De Witte

Published by Frank De Witte, 2026.

This is a work of fiction. Similarities to real people, places, or events are entirely coincidental.

THE CARTOGRAPHER OF FORGOTTEN FRONTS (BOOK I)

First edition. April 30, 2026.

ISBN: 979-8233602900

Written by Frank De Witte.

Table of Contents

"For those who look up when the smog parts."

"The war isn't about victory... it's about volume. The kinetic energy. The explosions. The screams. It keeps the ground shaking."

Chapter One

The Ink of Dead Empires

THE INK ON THE MAP was three hundred years old, but the blood was fresh.

Elian Vost sat in the high tower of the Hind Archive, a space that smelled of ozone, formaldehyde, and the slow, dry rot of history. It was a scent that had seeped into his clothes, his hair, and the very pores of his skin, the perfume of dead things. No matter how much he scrubbed his hands with rough soap, the fragrance remained.

Outside, the Smog Shield of the Citadel turned the midday sun into a bruise of sickly yellow light. It had been thirty years since the sun had truly touched the cobblestones of the inner courtyard. The people of the Hind didn't look up anymore; there was nothing to see but the ceiling of their own exhaust. They were a subterranean species living above ground, complexions the color of ash and just as damp.

Elian adjusted the brass lenses of his magnifier, the gears clicking softly in the silence. He dipped his nib into a pot of iron-gall ink, a mixture so biting it would eventually eat through the paper it lived on. He held the nib over the parchment. His hand, usually steady as stone, hovered with a slight tremor.

He was drawing a bridge.

It was a magnificent structure, the "Vrail Crossing," spanning the river Vrail in Sector Four. He etched the stone arches with practiced precision, shading the keystones to suggest weight and permanence. He drew the fortified toll houses on either bank, adding tiny loop-holes for imaginary muskets. He drew the little flags of the Hind Dominion fluttering in a wind that didn't exist.

It was a lie. A beautiful, meticulous, treasonous lie.

Elian knew the truth because he had seen the reconnaissance photos from a failed balloon probe three years ago. The Vrail River had dried up in the drought of '620. The bridge had been shelled into gravel during the Second Horn Offensive. There was no river. There was no bridge. There was only a jagged ravine filled with toxic mud, razor-wire, and the rusted skeletons of walkers that had marched into the gap and never marched out.

But the Ministry demanded a bridge. The Doctrine of Continuity stated that the Empire remained intact, and as a result, the Ministry enforced the use of maps from '600, before the major territorial losses. So Elian drew a bridge.

"It's wrong, Elian," a voice grumbled from the doorway.

Elian didn't look up. He finished the shading on the nonexistent archway, the rasp of the quill loud in the quiet room. "Of course it's wrong, Jarek. It's a map of a war that doesn't exist anymore."

Jarek stepped into the cramped office, ducking his head to avoid the bundles of drying herbs hanging from the rafters, Elian's futile attempt to mask the chemical stench. Jarek was a heavy-set logistics officer with skin like cured vellum, a byproduct of a life lived entirely under the smog. He dropped a heavy requisition form onto the drafting table. Dust motes danced in the impact, swirling in the shaft of yellow light.

"Command wants an update," Jarek said, wiping grease from his forehead with a rag that was equally grimy. "The supply trains are getting lost in Sector Four again. Drivers say the road just... ends."

"The road doesn't end," Elian corrected softly, finally looking up. He was a man of sharp angles and fingers stained black by his craft, looking younger than his forty years, though his eyes held the perpetual squint of someone trying to read in the dark. "The road was swallowed by the earth. The Horns mined the bedrock during the retreat of '680. The entire valley is a sinkhole now."

"Well, put the sinkhole on the map," Jarek snapped, his patience fraying. "My drivers are driving millions of rounds of ammo into a pit. We can't afford to feed the mud, Elian."

"I can't."

"Why? You're the Senior Cartographer. You have the pen. You have the seal."

"Because." Elian sighed, tapping the heavy crimson seal at the bottom of the parchment. It depicted the Iron Fist of the Hind, unyielding and eternal. "According to the Doctrine, we hold that road. If I draw a sinkhole, I am admitting we lost territory. That is defeatism. Defeatism is treason. And treason is a firing squad behind the chemical sheds."

Jarek rubbed his face, his exhaustion palpable. It wasn't just physical tiredness; it was the spiritual fatigue of a man whose job was to organize a disaster. "So the trains keep driving into the muck?"

"Until the war ends or the sinkhole fills up with trucks," Elian said, returning to his work. "I'd bet on the sinkhole."

This was the reality of the 700th year. The war had gone on for so long that it had detached itself from geography. It was no longer a contest of movement; it was a geological era. The Horns and the Hinds, the current "Orders" grinding against each other, were just the latest layer of sediment. Below them were the bones of the Molks and the Winders, and below them, things that didn't even have names. The war wasn't fighting for the world; it was the world.

Suddenly, the air in the room vibrated.

It wasn't a sound so much as a pressure change, a low-frequency thrum that rattled the inkpots on Elian's desk. The dust on the floor jumped, reorganizing itself into new patterns.

Jarek froze, his hand going instinctively to the sidearm he kept but had never fired. "Is that an incoming barrage? Horn Heavy Artillery?"

Elian tilted his head. He knew the sounds of the war like a conductor knows an orchestra. The Horn artillery was a rhythmic, thudding bass note, industrial and angry. The Hind return fire was a sharp, cracking tenor.

This was different. This was a smooth, tearing sound, terrifyingly organic, like silk being ripped by a god.

"No," Elian whispered, a strange chill walking up his spine. It felt like a memory of a sound he had never heard. "That's something else."

He moved to the slit window of the archive tower. Below, the vast, soot-stained courtyard of the Hind Citadel was usually a hive of activity. Conscripts marching in squares. Steam-trucks idling. The constant, hoarse shouting of drill sergeants trying to turn starving boys into iron men.

Now, it was silent. Thousands of soldiers had stopped dead. They were all looking up.

The smog was parting.

A ship was descending. It possessed no rivets, no smokestacks, and no visible engines belching black smoke. It was a teardrop of matte silver, silent and terrifyingly clean against the grime of the fortress. It hovered inches above the mud, defying the gravity that seemed to crush everything else in their world.

"The Recons," Jarek breathed, joining him at the window. "I thought they were a rumor from the West Coast. A ghost story."

"They're real," Elian murmured.

He watched as a ramp descended seamlessly from the silver hull. Figures emerged. They didn't wear the heavy, rusted plate armor of the Hind, nor the ragged leathers of the conscripts. They wore suits that shimmered, changing color to match the stone of the courtyard. They moved with a fluidity that suggested they weren't weighed down by the atmosphere, or by history.

Elian felt a sudden, violent pull in his chest. For twenty years, he had been a cartographer of lies, drawing borders that didn't exist for generals who would never leave their bunkers. But looking at that ship, he saw something he hadn't seen since he was a small child, back before the Smog Shield was finalized.

He saw Newness.

In a world where everything was repaired, scavenged, or inherited, the ship looked impossible. It looked like the future.

"They aren't here for the High Command," Elian realized aloud.

"What? Who else is there?" Jarek asked, squinting. "They're landing in the General's courtyard."

"Look at their equipment," Elian pointed. The figures weren't carrying rifles. They were carrying tripods, sensors, and optical devices. "They aren't soldiers, Jarek. They're surveyors."

Three hours later, the summons came.

Elian expected to be ignored. The Hinds were a hierarchy of heavy metal and blood; cartographers were considered little more than archivists, necessary furniture, like a filing cabinet or a coat rack. Yet, the heavy oak door of his office slammed open, and two Palace Guards filled the frame.

They were hulks of men, encased in steam-assist armor that hissed and vented heat with every movement. Their faces were hidden behind gas masks shaped like iron skulls, the standard issue of the Citadel Guard. They smelled of hydraulic fluid and intimidation.

"Cartographer Vost." The lead guard's voice was a metallic growl amplified by a speaker. "You are summoned to the Strategy Room."

Elian stood up, carefully wiping ink from his fingers with a rag. He didn't hurry. Dignity was the only currency he had left. "Am I under arrest?"

"You are required," the guard said. "Move."

The walk to the Strategy Room was a journey through the intestines of a dying beast. The Hind Citadel was a labyrinth of stone corridors designed to withstand orbital bombardment. The walls were lined with the statues of dead generals, their stone faces chipped and stained with residue. They passed infirmaries where the groans of the wounded echoed off the vaulted ceilings, a low, constant chorus of pain. Everywhere, there was the smell of unwashed bodies, burnt oil, and boiled cabbage. The lights flickered constantly. The Citadel's geothermal generators were failing, another secret kept by the Doctrine of Continuity.

They reached the heavy blast doors of the nerve center. Hydraulic locks groaned, ancient tumblers falling into place, and the doors swung open.

The Strategy Room was a cavernous hall dominated by a massive holographic table that flickered and buzzed with static. The air was cold, scrubbed by high-grade filters reserved for the elite. Around the table stood the Generals of the Hind. They looked like statues of iron and scar tissue, their uniforms heavy with medals for battles that had achieved nothing. They fell silent as Elian entered.

But Elian didn't look at them. He looked at the woman standing at the head of the table.

She was tall, wearing the shifting grey suit of the visitors. Her face was exposed. Pale, sharp, and terrifyingly calm. She had no cybernetics, no scars, no signs of the rot that afflicted everyone else. She looked like she had walked out of a laboratory, sterile and precise.

"This is the Archivist?" the woman asked. Her voice was clear, cutting through the low hum of the ventilation fans. She looked Elian up and down, taking in his stained fingers and the defiance in his posture.

General Korm, the Supreme Commander of the Hind forces, grunted. He was a massive man, half of his face replaced by a crude iron prosthetic that housed a glowing red ocular sensor. He leaned on the table, his knuckles white. "He is the Senior Cartographer. Vost. He knows the archives better than anyone."

The woman turned her gaze to Elian. It felt like being scanned by a machine. "I am Sub-Director Aphra of the Reconnaissance Initiative.

My people have traveled three thousand miles to bring an end to this conflict."

Elian didn't salute. He was too fascinated. "An end? The Horns won't surrender just because you have floating ships. They don't fight for territory anymore. They fight because fighting is what they do. It's their metabolism."

"We do not intend to fight the Horns," Aphra said coolly. "We intend to bypass them. But to do that, we need to understand the terrain." She gestured to the massive holographic table. "Show me the Frontline."

Elian approached the table. The holographic light washed out the color of his skin, turning him into a ghost. He looked at the jagged red line dividing the continent. A line he had redrawn a thousand times, always in the same place, always a lie.

"This," Elian said, pointing to the light, "is the Frontline according to the Ministry of Truth."

"It is accurate," General Korm barked, his mechanical eye whirring as it focused on Elian.

"It is a fiction," Elian said.

The silence that followed was heavy enough to crush a man. The other generals stiffened. To contradict Korm was usually a death sentence.

"Explain yourself, Cartographer," Korm growled, his hand resting on the heavy pistol at his belt. "Before I have you shot for sedition."

Elian looked at Aphra. He saw a flicker of interest in her cool eyes. She was testing him.

"General Korm fights on maps drawn in the year 600," Elian said, his voice steady despite the racing of his heart. "Since then, rivers have moved. Mountains have been flattened by orbital bombardment from the Winder era. Valleys have been filled with the wreckage of warmachines."

He reached into his coat pocket. The guards tensed, weapons raising. Elian pulled out a small, leather-bound notebook. It was battered, held together with twine.

"This," Elian said, slamming the notebook onto the holographic table, "is the truth."

He opened it. Inside were not clean lines and stamps. They were charcoal sketches. Notes scribbled in the margins. Calculations of erosion rates and crater depths.

"The 'Frontline' isn't a line, Sub-Director," Elian said, looking Aphra in the eye. "It hasn't been a line for centuries. It is a wound. It is a scar that is five hundred miles wide and seven hundred years deep."

Aphra picked up the notebook. She ran a gloved finger over the charcoal smudge of a massive crater labelled The Grave of Sector 7.

"A scar," she repeated softly.

"A No Man's Land," Elian corrected. "Nobody knows what is in there anymore. The Horns stay on their side, we stay on ours, and we shell the middle. But the middle has grown wild. The geography is... aggressive."

Aphra tapped a console on her wrist. "Our sensors indicate high-energy signatures in that zone. Anomalies. We cannot deploy our stabilization tech if we are flying blind. We need a path through the scar."

She looked at Korm, then back to Elian. "General Korm says you're a traitor for suggesting the maps are wrong. I think you're just the only one who admits we're blind."

"I'm not blind," he whispered. "And I'm certainly not lost. I am just the only one who isn't closing his eyes."

"Then find us," Aphra said. She placed a device on the table. A small, metallic sphere that hovered and projected a beam of pure white light. "We are assembling an expedition. Not an army. A survey team. We go into the No Man's Land. We map the terrain, we locate the old Winder ruins, and we find a path to the Horn Citadel to force a ceasefire."

"You want me to go into the Grey Zone?" Elian laughed, a dry, brittle sound. "That's a death sentence. The radiation alone..."

"We have technology to suppress the radiation," Aphra interrupted. "But we do not know the history. We do not know the landmarks of the old wars. You do."

She leaned in, her voice dropping to a whisper that the Generals couldn't hear. "There are things in the dark, Cartographer. Machines left behind by the Molks that are still dreaming. If we wake them, this war won't last another 700 years. It will end in an hour."

Elian looked at the holographic table. He looked at the vast, blank space between the red lines. The Terra Incognita. For his entire life, he had drawn lines on paper, tracing the borders of a cage. Now, someone was offering him the key to open the door and step into the dark.

"I need my equipment," Elian said, his voice trembling slightly. "And I need access to the Restricted Archives before we leave."

Aphra smiled, a sharp, dangerous expression. "Granted. Pack your instruments, Cartographer. Tomorrow, we redraw the world."

Chapter Two

The Silence of the Grey

THE STAGING GROUND for the expedition was an insult to the architecture of the Citadel. In the center of the outer courtyard, amidst the heavy, soot-stained granite and iron gargoyles, the Recons had erected a bubble of pure white light.

It wasn't canvas or glass; it was a localized containment field that hummed with a frequency that made Elian's teeth ache.

He stood awkwardly in the center of it, clutching his canvas satchel to his chest like a shield. The air inside the bubble was scrubbed, recycled, and aggressively odorless. It smelled of absolutely nothing, which, to a man used to the scent of ozone and wet wool, felt like a void.

Around him, Recon technicians moved with fluid, silent grace. They wore skinsuits that shimmered like oil on water, their faces hidden behind smooth, featureless faceplates. Instruments floated in the air without support, calibrating themselves with soft, melodic chimes.

"You cannot wear wool into the Zone, Cartographer," a technician said. Her voice didn't come from a mouth; it was projected directly into his ear from a speaker in the wall. "It is porous. It holds radiation, biological spores, and particulate toxins. It is a sponge for death."

Elian looked down at his coat. It was heavy, scratchy wool, dyed the dark green of the Hind logistics corps. It was patched at the elbows with leather and smelled of pipe tobacco, old dust, and the ink he used to draw lies. It was the smell of safety.

"It holds my compass. My charcoal. It has pockets," Elian muttered defensively, tightening his grip on the strap. "I need pockets."

"The suit has storage integration," the technician countered, stepping forward with a bundle of opalescent grey fabric. "And it will keep your blood inside your body if the pressure drops. Your coat will not."

Reluctantly, Elian stripped.

He felt absurdly vulnerable, a soft, pale creature of the archives exposed to the sterile glare. He was a man of paper and ink in a room of light and energy. When he pulled on the Recon suit, it didn't just fit; it adhered. It tightened instantly against his skin, warm and weightless. It felt less like clothing and more like he had been dipped in liquid mercury.

"Vital signs sync," a cool voice chimed in his ear, startling him. "Heart rate elevated. Cortisol levels high. Adrenaline detected."

"I'm fine," Elian snapped at the air, reaching for his satchel. "I'm just allergic to the future."

"That equipment is redundant," Sub-Director Aphra said, appearing at the edge of the bubble. She was fully suited now, her helmet retracted to reveal her sharp, calculating face. Her hair was pulled back tight, severe and practical. "Our sensors map terrain in real-time down to the millimeter. You do not need charcoal and dead wood."

Elian slung the heavy canvas strap over his shoulder. The rough texture of the bag against the sleek suit felt grounding. "Your sensors see what is there, Sub-Director. My maps remind me of what used to be there. The geography of this war is half memory. I'm keeping it."

Aphra stared at him for a beat, her eyes scanning him as if he were a glitch in the code. Then, she gave a curt nod. "Sentimental. But perhaps necessary. Boarding in two minutes."

The transport vehicle, they called it a "Skiff", sat on the mud like a silver tear shed by a giant. It was a sliver of burnished metal that looked too fragile for war. It possessed no treads to crush the earth nor wheels to grind it. It hummed with a magnetic repulsion that pushed the mud away in concentric ripples, hovering six inches off the ground.

There were five of them: Aphra, Elian, two Recon guards carrying rifles that looked more like surgical instruments than weapons, and a pilot who was wired directly into the ship's console via a bundle of glowing cables at the base of his skull.

They slipped out of the Citadel gates just as the dawn broke through the smog layer.

Passing the Hind Defensive Line was like sailing past the carcass of a dead god. Massive artillery cannons, the size of skyscrapers, rusted in the gloom. They were manned. Elian saw the flicker of cooking fires in the gun nests and the laundry hanging from the barrels. But, they hadn't fired in decades. The soldiers looked down from the parapets at the silent, metallic Skiff. Their faces were hollow, their eyes dark pits of boredom and malnutrition. They were ghosts haunting a graveyard of iron.

Then, they passed the last bunker. The concrete gave way to blasted earth.

"Crossing the Zero Line," the pilot announced, his voice flat and synthesized.

Elian flinched. He expected a wall of fire. He expected the roaring shelling that he had heard in the distance since he was a boy, the thunder that rattled the windows of the archives.

Instead, there was silence.

The No Man's Land (the Grey Zone) was not a desert. It was a jungle of trauma.

The earth had been churned so many times by high explosives that the soil itself had changed color, turning a bruised, necrotic purple-grey. From this toxic mulch, strange flora had erupted. Trees with bark like iron slag twisted toward the sky, their leaves pale and translucent as skin. Vines pulsed with a faint, bioluminescent thrum, wrapping around the shattered skeletons of tanks that had died three hundred years ago.

"Atmospheric scrubbers active," Aphra said, her voice filtered through the comms. "The air out here is forty percent heavy metals. Without the suit, your lungs would crystallize in an hour."

"It's... quiet," Elian whispered. He pressed his face to the glass, his breath fogging the pristine surface. "Where are the craters? The fire?"

"The earth heals," Aphra said, though she sounded disgusted by it. She tapped her screen, analyzing the soil composition. "It consumes the war and grows over it. It's a scab."

"It's not a scab," Elian corrected, pointing to a depression in the landscape that looked like a thumbprint pressed into wet clay. "That valley? That was the Battle of the Third Interregnum. Ten thousand men died there in a single afternoon. The soil isn't purple because of chemicals, Aphra. It's purple because it's been fed."

Aphra looked at him, her brow furrowing. "You romanticize the slaughter, Cartographer."

"I catalog it," Elian said. "There is a difference. You see data. I see ghosts."

They traveled for two hours, deeper than any Hind patrol had gone in a century. The Skiff glided over marshes where the water was thick and oily, bubbling with unknown chemistry.

"Stop," Elian said suddenly.

Aphra looked at him. "We are on a schedule, Vost. We are mapping the route to the Horns."

"Stop the ship!" Elian insisted, pointing a shaking finger at a ridge rising from the purple undergrowth. "That. Do your sensors see that?"

"It registers as a geological anomaly," the pilot said. "High silicon content. No heat signature."

"It's not geological," Elian said, grabbing his charcoal. "Set us down."

Aphra signaled the pilot. The Skiff settled with a soft hiss. The ramp lowered, and the smell of the Zone hit them; even through the suit's filters, Elian tasted copper and ozone. It tasted like blood on a battery.

He stumbled down the ramp, his boots sinking into the spongy moss. He walked toward the ridge.

Up close, the material wasn't just rock. It was a seamless, singing silicate glass. It was opaque, swirling with frozen patterns of immense heat. It wasn't natural. It curved.

"A Winder ship," Elian breathed. He ran a gloved hand over the surface. It was cold, colder than the air. "They fell from the sky during the Second Interregnum. The Hinds say they were demons. The archives say they were orbital bombers."

"It's massive," Aphra said, stepping up beside him. She tapped her wrist console, scanning the structure. "The material is absorbing our active scans. It's... humming. Radiometric dating places it here... six hundred years?"

"At least," Elian said. He opened his satchel and began to sketch the curve of the hull, trying to capture the way the alien vines were struggling to grip the smooth surface. "This proves it. The Winders weren't a myth. They were technologically superior to us, and they still lost."

"Lost to whom?" Aphra asked, looking at the smooth, unbroken hull.

"To the Molks," Elian said, pointing at the ground. "Look at the fracture pattern at the base. This ship didn't crash. It was pulled down. Something from below grabbed it and crushed the engines."

Aphra looked disturbed for the first time. She motioned to her guards. "Set up a perimeter. Scan the subsurface."

Elian continued to sketch, losing himself in the lines. He felt a strange thrill. He was the first cartographer to document a Winder hull in centuries. He was filling in the blank space. He was correcting the lie.

Then, the hair on his arms stood up.

It wasn't a sound. It was a sensation of being observed. A pressure on the back of his neck, like the air itself had gained weight.

Elian paused, his charcoal hovering over the paper. He slowly turned his head, scanning the line of twisted slag-trees fifty yards away. The mist was thick there, curling around the trunks like grey fingers.

"Sub-Director," Elian said, his voice low.

"I see the thermal readings," Aphra said, her voice tight. "Guard One, Sector North. Movement."

"I don't see anything," the guard replied, raising his rifle. "Thermals are cold. Motion is zero."

Elian squinted. There, between two iron-bark trees. A shadow.

But it wasn't shaped like a man. It was tall, impossibly thin, and it seemed to... flicker. It mimicked the sway of the trees, but the rhythm was wrong, like a film reel missing every third frame. It was a jagged, halting motion.

"It's watching us," Elian whispered.

"Is it a scout? A Horn patrol?" Aphra demanded, her hand going to her sidearm.

"No." Elian backed away, clutching his sketchbook to his chest. "Horn soldiers breathe. That thing... it's just standing there. It's vibrating."

The shadow shifted. It didn't walk; it seemed to dissolve and reform a few feet closer.

"Warning." The pilot's voice crackled over the comms, panic bleeding into the synthetic tone. "Gravimetric shear detected. Power cells are rapidly depleting. Something isn't just draining us. It's feeding."

"Back to the ship," Aphra ordered, her composure cracking. "Now!"

They scrambled up the ramp. Elian took one last look back. The shadow had vanished. But on the smooth, glass surface of the Winder ship, a single, muddy handprint was slowly fading away.

The hand had six fingers.

As the ramp sealed and the Skiff surged upward, escaping the heavy gravity well of the crash site, Elian looked at his drawing. In his haste, he had sketched the tree line.

In the charcoal smudges, the figure was there. And it looked like it was waiting.

Chapter Three

The Ministry of Rust

JAREK WATCHED FROM the slit window of the Archive tower as the silver Skiff vanished into the smog like a needle slipping into grey wool. He felt a heavy, greasy stone of envy settle in his gut. Elian was gone. The Cartographer had been lifted out of the mud by visitors in climate-controlled suits, leaving Jarek behind to count the beans of the apocalypse.

"Lucky bastard," Jarek muttered, his breath fogging the cold glass.

He turned away from the window. The office felt smaller without Elian. It smelled of ozone and the peppermint tea Elian used to drink to settle his stomach. Now, without the tea to mask it, the room just smelled of old paper and the pervasive, metallic stink of the Citadel. The scent of a machine that hadn't been oiled in a century.

Jarek didn't have time for envy. The war didn't stop just because an airship landed.

He picked up his stamp. A heavy brass block with the word ALLOCATED on the bottom, and trudged down the spiral stairs. He didn't go to the map room. He went deeper, past the strategy decks and the barracks, down into the bowels of the Citadel, to the Logistics Hub.

If the Strategy Room was the brain of the Hind, the Logistics Hub was its gut. It was a cavernous, subterranean hall filled with the roar of steam pipes and the shouting of a thousand clerks. Pneumatic tubes hissed overhead like a frantic circulatory system, carrying requisition forms like blood cells. The air was hot, recycled, and tasted of sweat, cheap tobacco, and the copper tang of anxiety.

Jarek reached his desk, a fortress of paperwork stacked high enough to block out the flickering electric lights.

"Officer Jarek!"

The shout came from the front of the queue. Standing there, covered in mud that had dried to the consistency of concrete, was a Trench Sergeant. He was missing an ear, the scar tissue pink and shiny against his sallow skin. His armor was a patchwork of three different eras. A breastplate from the '600s, a pauldron from the '400s, and a helmet that looked like it had been hammered out of a cooking pot.

"Sergeant Kolver." Jarek sighed, sitting down. The chair groaned under his weight. "You're back early. Sector Four wasn't due for rotation until Tuesday."

"Sector Four is a swimming pool." Kolver slammed a heavy wooden crate onto Jarek's desk. The wood cracked under the impact. "We can't fight in it. The pumps failed. Again."

"I sent replacement gaskets last week," Jarek said, reaching for a form without looking up.

"You sent us cardboard soaked in wax!" Kolver roared. He pried the lid off the crate with a combat knife. "Look at this. Look at what you're sending my boys."

Jarek looked. Inside the crate were rows of artillery shells. They looked ancient. The brass casings were dull, covered in micro-fractures and ugly weld marks where they had been resized.

"Class-C ordnance," Jarek recited, his voice flat. "Refilled. Standard issue for defensive lines."

"Refilled?" Kolver picked up a shell and held it to the flickering light. "This casing has been fired five times, Jarek. Look at the stamps. 'Year 698'. 'Year 699'. 'Year 700'. It's been welded so many times it's oval. It doesn't even fit the breech."

He slammed the shell back down.

"Three of my gunners died yesterday. Not from Horn snipers, but from this."

"The breech exploded when they tried to fire. You aren't sending us ammo; you're sending us bombs that go off in our faces."

Jarek looked at the Sergeant's shaking hands. He then looked at the line of soldiers behind him, men and women in patched armor, holding rifles held together with wire and prayer. They didn't look like an army; they looked like scavengers who had stolen uniforms. Their eyes were hollow, stripped of hope, filled only with the dull persistence of the doomed.

"I don't have Class-A," Jarek said quietly. "The Factory... the Deep Supply... it hasn't sent a shipment of new brass in six months."

"Then where is it going?" Kolver demanded. "The General's Guard has new gear. The Palace Police have shiny boots."

"They get the trickle," Jarek said, his voice dropping to a whisper. "We get the rust. That's the Doctrine, Kolver. We maintain. We recycle. We endure."

"We die," Kolver corrected. He leaned in, smelling of wet earth and unwashed fear. "The Horns... they're screaming over the radio. They say the 'Deep Ones' are starving. They're getting desperate. Last week, they charged our line with bayonets because they ran out of power cells. We beat them to death with shovels because our rifles jammed. It's not a war anymore, Jarek. It's a brawl in a graveyard."

Jarek looked at the requisition form Kolver had slammed down. Request: 5,000 Rounds, Class-A. High Velocity.

He picked up his stamp. The brass felt cold and heavy, like a weapon.

DENIED.

He stamped the paper. The sound was like a gunshot in the crowded room.

"I can give you Class-D," Jarek said, hating the words as they left his mouth. "Refilled seven times. Powder load reduced by twenty percent to prevent bursting."

Kolver stared at him. The hate in the Sergeant's eyes wasn't sharp anymore; it was dull, exhausted. "That won't penetrate Horn heavy coats."

"Aim for the eyes," Jarek said mechanically. "It's all I have."

Kolver grabbed the form, spat on the floor, and marched away.

Jarek slumped in his chair. This was the secret war. Not the one Elian drew on maps with neat red lines. This was the war of attrition where victory wasn't measured in miles taken, but in how many days you could make a pair of boots last before the rot set in.

"Attention." The loudspeakers crackled overhead, the voice tinny and distorted. "Victory Report. General Korm announces the strategic containment of the Northern Salient. The Doctrine of Continuity holds strong. Production quotas are met. Praise the Iron."

"Lies," Jarek whispered.

He pulled a ledger from his bottom drawer. The real ledger, bound in black leather, not the one he showed the Ministry inspectors.

Steel Reserves: Critical. Nitrates: Critical. Medical Supplies: Exhausted.

He looked at the numbers. They didn't add up to Continuity. They added up to zero. The Hind war machine wasn't a juggernaut; it was a corpse running on galvanic reflex.

"Run, Elian," Jarek thought, looking up at the stained ceiling tiles, imagining the silver ship breaking through the clouds into the sunlight he couldn't remember. "Don't come back. There's nothing left here but rust."

He dipped his pen into the ink, recycled soot mixed with water, and turned to the next soldier in line.

"Name and rank," Jarek said. "And tell me what you broke."

Chapter Four

The Gravity of Silence

THE SILVER SKIFF WAS dragged from the sky with a final, shuddering vibration, falling into the Grey Zone like a spent shell caught in the planet's heavy, invisible grip. One moment, the vessel was fighting for altitude, its magnetic engines screaming against a sudden, unseen anchor. The next, the hum died instantly. The lights on the console didn't flicker; they simply ceased. There was no explosion, no sparks. The ship simply became five tons of dead metal in a world that wanted to pull it down.

They fell fifty feet. It wasn't a long drop, but without the inertial dampeners, it felt like being thrown off a building inside a steel drum.

The impact didn't crunch; it squelched.

The Skiff slammed into the deep, bruised mud of the No Man's Land. The vessel tipped forward, burying its nose with a wet, sucking sound that vibrated through the hull like a throat clearing. Then, silence. Absolute, ringing silence.

Elian groaned, hanging sideways in his restraints. He tasted copper. He had bitten his tongue. He fumbled for the buckle, his hands shaking. The darkness inside the cabin was total, save for the rapidly fading luminescence of the control panels, dying like embers in water.

"Status." Aphra's voice cut through the dark. It was tight, controlled, but Elian could hear the strain of a woman trying to command a situation that had just defied the laws of physics.

"Systems dead," Marston reported from the back. "Emergency lighting is... negative. Batteries are drained. Completely flat."

"That's impossible," Aphra snapped, the sound of her tapping on a dead console echoing in the small space. "The backup cells are chemically isolated. They can't be drained. Cycle the reactor."

"They're empty, Sub-Director. Cold."

Elian managed to pop his buckle. He fell awkwardly against the bulkhead, his Recon suit stiffening on impact to protect his ribs. He scrambled up, looking toward the cockpit.

"Kaelen?" Aphra called out. "Get us back in the air."

There was no answer from the pilot's cradle.

"Kaelen!" Aphra moved to the front, cracking a chemical glow-rod. The harsh blue light washed over the pilot's chair, casting long, jagged shadows against the canopy.

Elian froze. Kaelen was still strapped in, the neural interface cables snaking from the dead console into the ports at the base of his skull. But his body was rigid, arched back as if in the grip of a seizure. His jaw was locked open in a silent scream, and his eyes were rolled back so far only the whites were visible.

"He's seizing," Elian said, scrambling forward. "Get him out!"

"Disconnect him," Aphra ordered Marston.

"He's clamped," Marston grunted, struggling with the locking mechanism. "The interface... it's locked down. The safety release isn't responding."

"It's not the chair," Elian realized, looking at the cables. They were pulsing faintly, a rhythmic, violet throb traveling from the ship into the pilot. "The ship isn't dead. It's feeding him into something."

"Cut them," Aphra said ruthlessly, drawing a vibro-knife from her belt.

"That could lobotomize him!" Marston protested.

"Leaving him connected is killing him! Do it!"

Marston slashed through the shielded conduits. A spark of blue feedback snapped, loud as a pistol shot. Kaelen convulsed violently, then slumped forward, held up only by his harness. He let out a long, rattling breath. He didn't speak; he just shivered, a low, constant vibration that rattled his teeth.

"Get him up," Aphra commanded, her face pale in the blue light. "Vost, blow the door. We're sinking."

Elian looked at the viewport. The glass was pitch black. The mud was rising, covering the windows. The ship was being swallowed by the earth. He hauled on the manual release lever. It groaned, metal grinding against metal. The suction of the muck outside was immense.

"Help me!" Elian grunted, bracing his feet against the wall.

Marston grabbed the lever with him. Together, they heaved. With a wet pop, the seal broke. The door didn't swing open; it fell, turning into a ramp that squelched into the mire.

The air of the Zone rushed in. It didn't smell like air. It smelled of wet iron, ancient rot, and electricity. It tasted like licking a battery.

They scrambled out onto the hull of the sunken ship. The Skiff was already waist-deep. The "mud" wasn't just dirt; it was a slurry of oil, water, and grey ash that clung to their boots like tar.

"Deploy the drones," Aphra ordered as they waded to a patch of solid ground, a ridge of fused rock that looked suspiciously like a spinal column. "I want a perimeter and a topological scan."

"Trying, Ma'am," Marston said. He pulled a silver sphere from his pack and tossed it into the air. The drone buzzed to life. It rose three feet, stabilized... and then dropped like a stone. It splashed into the sludge and sank without a bubble.

"Physics failure," Marston muttered, tapping his wrist readout frantically. "Local gravity is... fluctuating. It's spiking to three Gs in random pockets. The gyros can't compensate. Nothing flies here."

"We're blind," Aphra realized. She looked at her wrist comp. The holographic map was a fuzz of static. "The magnetic interference is jamming the satellite link. I can't see the terrain."

She looked at the horizon. The sun was setting, casting long, bruised shadows across the landscape. The "Slag Garden" stretched out before them. A nightmare forest where the trees were petrified twists of artillery barrels fused with iron-wood, and the undergrowth was a tangle of wire-grass that hissed in the wind.

"Not blind," Elian said.

He was kneeling on the rock, his satchel open. He held a simple, rusted iron compass in his hand. Amidst the chaos of the Recon's dying sensors, the analog needle trembled, fought the magnetic anomalies, and stubbornly settled back to a specific point.

"Magnetic North is still North," Elian said, looking up at her. "The planet hasn't stopped spinning just because you lost your batteries."

Aphra looked at the primitive device with a mix of disdain and desperation. "That thing is accurate to within... what? Five degrees?"

"It's accurate enough to keep us from walking in circles," Elian said. "Which is what your digital map is doing right now."

Aphra looked at the darkening sky. "The suit thermals are dropping. We can't stay in the open. The night temperature in the Zone drops to minus forty. If the cold doesn't kill us, the radiation pooling in the low ground will."

"We need shelter," Elian said. He pulled out his charcoal sketch. The one he had made of the Winder ship. He turned the paper over and began to draw a new map, using the compass and his own memory of the old Hind geological surveys. "The Doctrine of Continuity says the Molks built deep. They were burrowers."

"The Molks are a myth used to scare conscripts," Aphra said dismissively, checking Kaelen's pulse. The pilot was catatonic, his eyes tracking something in the sky that no one else could see.

"The Winder ship wasn't a myth," Elian countered, his voice sharp. "And neither was the thing that pulled it down."

He stood up, pointing a charcoal-stained finger toward a looming cliff face about two miles east. It was a black, jagged wall against the purple sky, darker than the surrounding night.

"There," Elian said. "The tectonic plates here are artificial. That cliff isn't natural uplift. It's a structure. It's our only chance."

Aphra hesitated. Her technology, the foundation of her entire worldview, was dead weight. She looked at the spot where the drone had sunk. She looked at the compass in Elian's hand.

"Two miles," Aphra calculated, looking at the treacherous terrain of the Slag Garden. "In this terrain, carrying Kaelen... that's an hour. Maybe two."

"Then we better start walking," Elian said.

He turned to lead the way, but a sound stopped him. A low, vibrating hum that seemed to come from the wreckage of the Skiff behind them. Elian turned back. In the distance, near where the Skiff had gone down, a blue light flickered. It was the glow of the Skiff's emergency beacon, finally activating in the mud.

But something was standing in front of it.

A shadow. Tall, impossibly thin, and flickering like a bad transmission. It wasn't just blocking the light; it was drinking it. The blue glow didn't cast a silhouette; it was absorbed into the entity, swirling inside it like ink in water.

"It followed us," Marston whispered, raising his rifle.

"Don't shoot," Elian hissed, grabbing the barrel. "It feeds on energy. You fire that thing, you're just feeding it dinner."

The Shadow turned. It didn't have eyes, but Elian felt the weight of its attention slam into him. The temperature dropped ten degrees in a second. Frost bloomed on the rocks at their feet.

"Run," Elian said, his voice trembling. "Don't look back. Just run."

They scrambled off the ridge and into the twisted iron forest of the Slag Garden, the darkness at their heels hungry and rising.

Chapter Five

The Rain of Teeth

THEY RAN UNTIL THEIR lungs burned, putting distance between themselves and the dying blue light of the Skiff. But the No Man's Land did not allow for simple flight.

The terrain was a graveyard of geology. Elian's boot broke through a patch of deceptive moss, plunging his leg knee-deep into a pocket of acidic slurry. He hissed in pain, the heat of it searing against the synthetic fibers of his Recon suit. He dragged himself out with a wet, sucking sound. The silver polymer smoked, pitting slightly, but the seal held.

"Hold," Aphra ordered, stumbling to a halt near a twist of fused iron that looked like a calcified ribcage. She tapped frantically at her wrist display. The holographic map flickered, dissolving into a storm of white static. "The magnetic interference is spiking. My sensors can't distinguish between the terrain and the background radiation. It's all just... noise."

"Your sensors are looking for geometry," Elian panted, scraping the toxic mud off his leg with his knife. "There is no geometry here, Sub-Director. Only erosion."

He looked up at the sky. The heavy, bruised clouds that permanently blanketed the Zone were churning. They weren't moving with the wind; they were boiling, turning a sickly, translucent shade of iodine-yellow.

"Barometer is dropping," Elian said, tapping the glass of his analog wrist-compass. The needle was spinning lazily, confused by the metal in the earth, but he wasn't looking at the needle. He was looking at the air pressure gauge. "Fast. Too fast."

"A storm?" Marston asked. He scanned the horizon with his rifle, his movements twitchy. He was looking for the Shadow they had fled from, but the dark remained empty.

"Not water," Kaelen whispered. The pilot was supported by Davis, his head lolling, eyes squeezed shut as if the grey light hurt them. "It tastes like copper," Kaelen mumbled, his tongue darting out to wet dry lips. "It tastes like old pennies."

Elian sniffed the air. Kaelen was right. The ozone smell of the crash was gone, replaced by a sharp, metallic tang that coated the back of his throat. He looked at the twisted shapes of the Slag Garden. Trees made of fused metal and petrified bone. He then realized what the yellow clouds meant. He had read about this in the oldest, most forbidden texts of the Hind archives, the ones bound in lead.

"Cover!" Elian shouted, panic sharpening his voice into a weapon. "We need hard cover! Now!"

"What is it?" Aphra demanded, moving to help Davis with the pilot.

"Corrosive hail," Elian yelled, pointing toward a ridge of jagged, rusted metal. The skeletal remains of a massive carrier ship half-buried in the mud. "The clouds are full of particulate metal and acid from the factory exhaust. It's not going to rain water; it's going to rain teeth!"

They sprinted toward the wreckage. The wind picked up instantly, screaming through the wire-grass like a thousand flutes out of tune. The first drop hit Marston's shoulder plate. It didn't splash; it pinged. Then it hissed. The advanced polymer of the Recon suit smoked, a black pockmark appearing on the white armor.

"Movement! Three o'clock!" Marston shouted, swinging his rifle.

Elian glanced back. Emerging from the fog, loping low to the ground, were shapes. They looked like wolves, but they moved with a jarring, mechanical gait. Their fur was matted with oil, and their skin was studded with shards of shrapnel that had embedded and healed over, turning them into living fragmentation grenades.

"Scrap-Hunters." Elian identified them, his hand going to the flare gun in his belt. "Mutated fauna. They hunt during the storms because their prey is pinned down."

"Open fire!" Aphra ordered, drawing her sidearm.

Marston leveled his rifle. A beam of coherent light slashed through the gloom. One of the wolves was hit mid-leap. The energy bolt burned a hole through its flank, sealing the wound instantly. The creature didn't even slow down; it didn't bleed. It just snarled, exposing teeth that looked like serrated obsidian.

"They have heavy metal deposits in their hides!" Aphra shouted, firing three rapid shots that sparked uselessly off the alpha's shoulder. "The energy is dispersing! Use kinetics! Aim for the eyes!"

"I don't have kinetics!" Davis yelled, struggling to keep Kaelen upright while fumbling for his weapon. "Standard loadout is energy!"

The wolves sensed the weakness. They didn't growl; they made a sound like grinding gears. They lunged at the slowest target. Davis screamed as the alpha clamped its jaws onto his armored forearm. The suit held for a second, then crunched under the pressure of jaws designed to crush bone and steel alike. Blood sprayed, dark and red against the white armor.

"There are too many!" Elian grabbed Aphra's arm, hauling her toward the gap in the hull of the ancient wreck. "Inside! The storm will kill them if we don't!"

"Davis!" Aphra screamed.

Marston was firing wildly, trying to drive the pack back. "Go! I've got him!"

"He's dead if we stay!" Elian shoved Aphra toward the dark opening. He turned. He raised his flare gun, a relic of the Hind trench kit, and fired point-blank at the ground in front of the wolves.

The magnesium flare erupted in a blinding white star. It wasn't high-tech; it was raw chemical violence. The wolves yelped, blinded by the sudden intensity, and scrambled back into the fog. Marston grabbed Davis by his good arm, hauling him up. They sprinted after Elian and Aphra, diving into the hollow belly of the ancient wreck just as the sky tore open.

It sounded like a hammer hitting an anvil.

The hail wasn't ice; it was semi-solid pellets of acidic slush and heavy metals. It hammered the metal hull above them with a deafening roar, a cacophony that drowned out even Kaelen's whimpering. Outside, a Scrap-Hunter tried to pursue. A hailstone the size of a fist struck its spine. The creature's back broke with a wet crunch. Within seconds, the pack was obliterated, beaten into the mud by the sheer violence of the weather.

Inside the wreckage, the noise was deafening, but they were sheltered. Aphra activated a glow-rod, bathing the cramped space in blue light. They were huddled in what used to be a cargo bay. The air was stale, smelling of centuries-old dust.

"Is everyone sealed?" Aphra asked, her voice shaking. She moved to Davis, checking the seal on his arm. The armor was punctured, blood leaking into the suit. The wolf bite was jagged, a mess of torn polymer and flesh.

"Suit integrity at ninety percent," Davis reported through gritted teeth as Marston applied a coagulant patch. "That rain... it eats poly-fiber."

"It eats everything," Elian said. He slid down the wall to sit on the floor, his chest heaving. "That's why the No Man's Land never heals. The weather keeps scrubbing the wound clean."

He looked around the space. The walls weren't riveted steel like Hind construction. They were smooth, seamless composite. And they were covered in writing. Strange, flowing script that looked less like language and more like musical notation was etched into the bulkhead.

"Winder script," Elian whispered. He reached out, tracing a groove with a trembling finger.

Aphra looked at him. She looked at his battered canvas satchel, his charcoal sticks, and the flare gun, a primitive chemical weapon still smoking in his hand.

"You knew," she said softly. "You smelled the air and knew it was acid. My atmospheric sensors just read 'precipitation'. My rifle barely scratched them. Your flare gun saved us."

"I read it," Elian corrected without looking up. He pulled out his notebook and began to sketch the Winder script. "In a book your 'new world' probably burned for fuel. You have satellites, Aphra. You have algorithms. But you don't have memory."

Kaelen groaned, shifting in his sleep. His eyes flickered open, but they weren't seeing the hull. "The noise..." he mumbled, clutching his head as the hail hammered the roof. "The sky is screaming... trying to drown out the Tone."

"What Tone?" Aphra asked, kneeling beside him. "The thunder?"

"No," Kaelen whispered, tears leaking from his eyes. "The song in the glass. The storm hates it. The storm wants to break the glass."

Aphra looked at her pilot, then back at Elian. The arrogance was gone from her face, replaced by a grim calculation. She was realizing that on this planet, survival wasn't about technology. It was about knowing which way the wind blew.

"We wait for the storm to pass," Aphra said, sitting down opposite Elian. She pulled a nutrient bar from her pack and offered him half. "And then, Cartographer... you teach me how to listen."

Chapter Six

The Carrion Market

THE STORM LASTED SIX hours. When it finally broke, it didn't leave a rainbow; it left the world glistening and steaming like a fever breaking. The acid had stripped the top layer of moss from the rocks, leaving the No Man's Land looking raw and red, like exposed meat under a permanent grey sky.

They moved out cautiously. The air was cleaner now, sharp and metallic, but the silence that followed the hail was unnerving.

"We need to find shelter before nightfall," Elian said, eyeing the darkening horizon. He checked his compass, but the needle was twitching violently, caught in a magnetic riptide. "The acid stripped the cover. If the temperature drops, we freeze. And we are walking on a magnetic fault line."

"We're being followed," Marston whispered from the rear guard position. He didn't raise his rifle; he knew better than to provoke a shadow in this place. "Not wolves. Bipeds."

Aphra signaled for a halt. She crouched behind a twist of slag that looked like a calcified lung, activating the thermal overlay on her visor. "I see them. Five... no, ten heat signatures. Low temperature. They're cold, barely above ambient."

"They're human," Elian said, peering over the rock. "Or they used to be."

Emerging from the steam were figures wrapped in layers of grey rags, plastic sheeting, and bits of old Hind armor that had been hammered flat to fit malformed limbs. They moved with a silent, shuffling efficiency. They weren't stalking the group; they were flanking them. They were dragging something. Monolithic rusted chains were slung over their shoulders, pulling a sled fashioned from a scorched car hood. On the sled lay the carcass of the Scrap-Hunter killed by the storm.

"Scavengers," Aphra said with distaste. "Grave robbers."

"Recyclers," Elian corrected, watching their movements. "And we aren't being hunted, Aphra. We're being herded."

"Herded where?"

"Look at the smoke." Elian pointed.

The figures were pushing them toward a depression in the ground. A monolithic crater fortified with sheets of corrugated iron and the serrated ribs of a dead Land-Crawler. Thick, greasy smoke curled from a central vent, smelling of burning plastic, roasted meat, and the ozone tang of arc-welding.

"A settlement," Elian breathed. "A static-point in the Zero Zone. I've seen mention of a 'black exchange' in the old logistics ledgers, but the Ministry claimed the area was sterilized. It shouldn't exist."

"We go around," Aphra said, her hand tightening on her sidearm. "We don't engage."

"We can't," Elian said. "Look at the terrain. They have the high ground and the numbers. Besides..." He tapped the glass of his compass. "The magnetic needle is spinning wild. There's a massive power source under that village. If there is a way to keep warm, it's through that smoke."

Aphra hesitated, looking at Kaelen, who was shivering violently despite the suit's heaters. "We need warmth," she admitted. "Weapons tight. But if they look at us wrong, drop them."

They descended into the crater.

The settlement was a nightmare of ingenuity, a shantytown built from the refuse of seven centuries of war. Huts were constructed from tank turrets and fused glass. Lanterns glowing with bioluminescent sludge hung from wires made of braided copper. It was a market, but they weren't just trading goods; they were trading survival.

Scavengers sat on rugs made of woven wire, displaying their wares. One man was selling batteries that leaked green fluid. Another was trading a pristine Horn officer's boot for a handful of rivets. A woman with no nose was carefully polishing a human skull, fitting it with a gas mask lens to create a bowl.

"The Carrion Market," Elian whispered. "The graveyard of every secret the Hind ever tried to bury."

As they entered the perimeter, the scavengers stopped their work. They didn't attack; they just stared. Their faces were hidden behind masks made from the skulls of local fauna or modified respirators that hissed with every breath.

A figure stepped forward from the central hut. A structure built from the hollowed-out skull of a Deep-Walker. He was tall, wearing a coat made entirely of stitched-together officer patches. Hind and Horn insignia mixed indiscriminately. He held a staff made from a Recon drone's antenna, likely from a probe lost decades ago.

"The Sky-Silver walks," the man rasped. His voice sounded like gravel in a mixer. He pointed his staff at Aphra. "Bad luck. Sky-Silver brings the heavy rain. Brings the rust."

"We are just passing through." Elian stepped forward, hands open, palms up. He switched to the guttural dialect of the Border Tribes. "We seek the heat. We trade words for warmth."

The leader tilted his head, the lenses of his mask whirring as they focused. "A Paper-Man? With the Sky-Silver? Strange pairing. Like a rat riding a hawk.

You have no metal, Paper-Man. What words do you have that are worth a thermal unit?"

Elian reached into his satchel. He didn't pull out a weapon; he pulled out a charcoal sketch. The drawing of the Winder Ship he had made earlier.

"I know where the Glass Sleeper lies," Elian said. "And I know the path through the acid-marshes that leads to it without tripping the mines."

The scavengers murmured. Information was currency here. A safe path to a new salvage site was worth more than gold. The leader snatched the paper, examining it before looking back at Elian.

"A good trade. For one hour of heat. No more."

"We need access to the vent," Elian pressed, ignoring the slight. "We need to go down."

The leader laughed, a dry, hacking sound. "Everyone goes down eventually, Paper-Man. We send the metal down. We send the meat down. The Deep Ones pay in heat."

He gestured to the center of the village. There, a monolithic, rusted grate covered a hole in the ground at least twenty feet wide. Warm air billowed up from it, keeping the crater habitable despite the freezing temperatures.

Around the grate, scavengers were working with a religious intensity, throwing scrap metal, helmets, rifles, pieces of the wolf, into the hole.

Clang. Clang. Clang.

They listened as the offerings hit something deep below. Seconds later, a heavy mechanical thud vibrated through the ground. A hiss of steam released from a valve, venting hot, moist air into the shivering crowd. The scavengers raised their hands to it, bathing in the exhaust like it was holy water.

"See?" The leader grinned beneath his skull mask. "We feed the mouth. The mouth breathes heat. Life for life. Metal for warmth."

Aphra grabbed Elian's arm, her grip tight. "Elian... look at the scrap they're throwing in. It's sorted."

Elian looked closer. It wasn't just random junk. There were piles: Ferrous. Non-ferrous. Biological. Even the Scrap-Hunter carcass was being stripped. Meat for the pot, bones and metal for the hole.

"It's not a religion," Elian realized, a cold dread settling in his stomach. "It's a hopper. A sorting chute."

"They're feeding a mechanism," Aphra whispered. "This isn't a ritual. It's a supply chain. They are the intake valves for the factory. But for what? What is still running down there that needs this much metal?"

"Can we use it?" Elian asked the leader.

"To go down?" The leader shrugged. "If you want to be slag, go ahead. But the Supervisors don't like live meat in the chute. It clogs the grinders."

"Supervisors?" Aphra asked.

The leader pointed to the edge of the crater, where the shadows of the ruins grew long. Standing there, perfectly still, was a tall, flickering silhouette. A Shadow.

It wasn't attacking the village. It was watching the work. It stood like an overseer, its form vibrating with a low, hungry hum. It was counting the scrap.

"They keep the tally," the leader said reverently. "If the tally is low... they take one of us to make up the weight."

Kaelen, who had been half-conscious, suddenly lifted his head. His eyes snapped open, reflecting the violet light of the entity. He looked at the Shadow, and the Shadow turned its faceless head toward him.

A vibration passed through the air. S sound that wasn't a sound, but a pressure on the brain.

"It knows me," Kaelen whispered, his voice trembling not with cold, but with recognition. "It says... the shift is starting. The quota must be met."

"We have to go," Aphra said, backing away from the grate. "This isn't an entrance. It's a garbage disposal."

"No," Elian said, looking at the Shadow, then at the grate. The heat rising from it was seductive, dangerous. "Every system has an intake. If we stay here, we freeze or we get added to the tally. If we want to survive the night, we have to follow the heat."

He looked at Aphra. "We jump."

Chapter Seven

The Throath of the World

THE FALL WAS SHORT, but the landing was brutal. They didn't hit stone; they hit a shifting mountain of rusted iron. Elian tumbled down a slope of jagged scrap, helmets, twisted rifles, and the calcified bones of machines, before slamming into a wall that vibrated with a dull, subterranean heat.

He gasped, the wind knocked out of him. The air here was thick, tasting of oil and old copper. It was hot. Suffocatingly so compared to the freezing surface of the Zone.

"Aphra?" he wheezed, fumbling for his glow-rod.

"Here." Her voice came from above, strangled with a rare note of panic. A beam of blue light cut through the rising dust. She was sliding down the scrap pile, dragging Kaelen with her.

Marston was already at the bottom, but he wasn't looking at them. He was staring back up toward the grate they had just vacated, his rifle raised, his chest heaving.

"Davis?" Elian asked, looking at the empty, shadowy space beside Marston. "Where is Davis?"

Marston lowered his rifle slowly. His face was pale beneath the grime. "He didn't make the jump. The Shadow... it grabbed his ankle. Just as he pushed off."

Aphra closed her eyes for a second, the guilt flashing across her face like a physical blow. "He was bleeding. The wolf bite. The Shadow smelled the leak."

"The Tally," Elian whispered, remembering the scavenger leader's words. "Life for heat. Davis paid our toll."

Above them, the grate remained silent. The Shadow didn't follow; it had taken its payment.

"We can't stay here," Marston said, his voice trembling with a mixture of fear and rage. "We're going to get buried."

Clang.

A monolithic piece of metal, a tank tread, fell from the grate above, bouncing off the far wall and landing inches from Elian's boot. The scavengers were back to work. The intake was active.

"The air is flowing that way." Elian pointed to a service archway half-buried in the debris. It was dark, but a steady draft of warm air was being sucked into it. "Ventilation return. It leads to the lungs."

They scrambled over the trash, slipping on loose casings and shattered glass. They squeezed through the archway just as another load of heavy scrap rained down behind them, filling the space where they had been standing with a thunderous crash.

The tunnel beyond was different. The chaos of the surface, the rust, the mud, the jagged edges, vanished instantly.

"Lights," Aphra ordered.

The beams revealed a corridor that defied logic. There were no rivets. No support beams. No dripping pipes. The tunnel was a perfect cylinder of smooth, dark stone, thirty feet high, sloping gently downward. It possessed a mathematical precision that felt hostile to the human eye, which instinctively sought the cracks and imperfections that simply weren't there.

"It's... clean," Marston whispered, running a gloved hand over the wall. He sounded disturbed.

"It's not just clean," Elian said, stripping off his heavy glove to touch the stone. It hummed against his palm. A faint, residual heat like a paved road after a long summer day. "It's active. This isn't a cave. It's a vein."

"Power," Kaelen murmured. The pilot pushed himself away from Aphra. He was walking on his own now, though his movements were jerky, like a marionette with tangled strings. He didn't look at the others; he looked down the throat of the tunnel. "The stone is awake. It tasted the metal we brought. It knows we are here."

They walked for twenty minutes, descending deeper into the planet's crust. The oppression of the rock above them, miles of it, began to weigh on their minds. The heat grew steady, a dry, electric warmth that dried the sweat on their skin.

"Halt," Aphra finally ordered. She leaned against the wall, sliding down until she was sitting. The exhaustion of the acid storm, the chase, and the loss of Davis had finally caught up to her. "We rest here for four hours. Vital signs are spiking. We need to lower our heart rates."

"Guard the rear," she told Marston. "Vost... figure out where we are."

They set up a makeshift camp in the center of the smooth corridor. It felt sacrilegious to eat nutrient paste in such a pristine place, like picnicking in a cathedral. Elian sat a little apart, leaning against the humming wall. He opened his satchel, miraculously intact, and noticed Aphra watching him. Her face was smeared with soot, her eyes haunted.

"You look comfortable," she said, her voice lacking its usual command.

"I'm used to basements," Elian said, offering her his water flask. "The Hind archives are deep underground. We find comfort in the weight of stone. It means the artillery can't reach us. Down here, the world makes sense."

Aphra took a drink, grimacing at the metallic taste. "It feels like a tomb."

"It's not," Elian corrected gently. "Tombs are for the dead. This place is... dormant. It's a waiting room." He gestured around them. "You didn't expect this, did you? The West has forgotten the Old Layers."

"The West has moved on," Aphra said defensively. "We rebuilt. We have cities of glass and light. We don't live in holes."

"Then why are you here?" Elian asked. "If your world is a paradise, why come to the slaughterhouse?"

Aphra looked at the nutrient tube in her hand. "Because glass is fragile, Vost. And stability is... stagnant. We haven't had a new invention in two hundred years. We haven't had a new philosophy. We call it 'The Great Plateau.'" She looked up, her eyes hard. "We came here because we thought the War was an engine of evolution. We thought we were the doctors coming to cure the patient."

She laughed bitterly. "Now I realize we might just be another virus. And Davis died for a geography lesson."

Elian looked at the floor. He noticed something in the texture of the stone. Faint, etched grooves that caught the light of the glow-rods. He pulled out a stick of charcoal and rubbed it directly onto the floor. As the black dust settled into the microscopic grooves, a pattern emerged.

Lines. Intersecting curves. Geometries that implied movement and velocity.

"It's not decoration," Elian realized, his heart beating faster. He scrubbed harder, revealing a map that stretched for ten feet. "It's a schematic. A transit map."

He looked down the tunnel with new eyes.

"This isn't a bunker, Aphra. It's a highway. The Molks moved underneath the crust. They could move armies from the Northern Salient to the Southern Coast without ever seeing the sky."

"If this tunnel connects to the network..." Aphra began.

"Then we can walk straight under the Frontline," Elian finished. "We can bypass the No Man's Land, the radiation, the trenches. We can pop up right inside Horn territory."

"Or it leads us straight into the Molk capital," Kaelen said.

The pilot was standing over the charcoal map. His eyes were no longer rolled back; they were focused, pinned with terrifying clarity on the darkness ahead. The veins in his neck were pulsing black.

"Kaelen?" Aphra asked, standing up slowly.

"The highway isn't empty," Kaelen whispered. He pointed a trembling finger down the tunnel. "I can hear the traffic."

Elian strained his ears. At first, there was nothing but the blood rushing in his own head. Then, he felt it in his teeth before he heard it. A low, rhythmic thrumming.

Thrum... Thrum... Thrum...

It wasn't mechanical. It was resonant. It vibrated through the soles of their boots like a low-voltage current. It sounded biological.

"Is it a train?" Marston asked, raising his rifle.

"No," Elian said, staring into the dark, terrified and exhilarated. "It sounds like a heartbeat."

Kaelen turned to them, a smile stretching his face that didn't reach his eyes. "The System is rebooting. We woke it up when we crashed. We rang the doorbell."

Aphra looked at Elian. "Pack the gear. Now."

"Forward is the only way," she continued. "If this is a transit system, there has to be a station. A control room."

As they marched deeper into the throat of the world, Elian looked at the floor. The charcoal dust on the map was vibrating, dancing into new patterns with every beat of the pulse below. The map was changing. The war was changing.

And for the first time in seven hundred years, the Molks were listening.

Chapter Eight

The Prayer of Gear

THE MOUNTAIN DID NOT speak often, but when it did, the Horns held their breath.

Kara stood on the grated walkway of the Receiving Bay, her knuckles white as she gripped the rusted railing. Below her, three thousand workers in yellow rubberized trench coats stood in absolute silence. They were looking up at the massive blast doors of the Main Shaft. The throat of the world that connected their Citadel to the Deep Ones below.

"Pressure rising," Jonas whispered. He didn't look at the brass gauge on the wall. He was clutching his temples, his eyes squeezed shut against a pain that seemed to radiate from his very teeth. He had lived with this "static" his whole life, a phantom frequency the priests called a curse. "It's coming. I can... I can feel the friction in the rock."

"Put your mask on, Jonas," Kara snapped, noticing the way he swayed. She assumed it was just the tremors of the mountain; Jonas had always been sensitive to the machine's moods. "The vents leak when the shaft opens. You want sulfur in your lungs?"

Jonas scrambled to pull his mask up, but his hands shook. He could hear the hum of the deeper gears, a sound no one else noticed, vibrating through the soles of his boots seconds before the physical mechanisms even engaged. To him, the mountain wasn't just stone; it was a broadcast.

Kara checked her clipboard, ignoring the boy's discomfort.

Shift 4 Manifest: Expected: 500 Crates (Class-A Munitions). Expected: 200 Units (Power Cells). Expected: 50 Units (Nutrient Paste).

It was a wish list. She knew it. The Deep Ones hadn't sent a full shipment in her lifetime.

"Brothers and Sisters!" A voice boomed from the pulpit, a suspended cage of iron hanging above the shaft like a spider's egg sac.

It was a Gear-Priest, his red robes heavy and stiff with layers of "sacred" grease. His face was hidden behind a gold mask shaped like a multi-lensed insect, designed to filter out doubt as much as toxins. He swung a censer, filling the bay with the acrid, stinging smoke of burning transmission fluid.

"The gears turn!" the Priest shrieked, his voice amplified by the megaphones bolted to the cavern walls. "The Great Machine remembers us! We have bled for the Line! We have starved for the Line! And now, the Deep Ones reward our faith!"

The workers murmured, a low tide of desperate hope. They clasped their hands, some missing fingers, some wrapped in oily rags, and bowed their heads. They looked less like soldiers and more like pilgrims at the end of a death march.

Clang.

The sound echoed like a gunshot in a cathedral. For Jonas, the noise was a physical blow to the back of his skull. He gasped, dropping to one knee as the locking clamps on the blast doors disengaged. The mountain groaned, a deep, subsonic vibration that rattled teeth and loosened centuries of soot from the ceiling.

Kara didn't pray. She watched the chains. She counted the links as they passed the winch. Too fast, she thought, her mind calculating the tension. The counterweight is dropping too fast. There's no load.

Massive links, each as thick as a man's torso, began to move, grinding against dry tumblers. The blast doors hissed open, revealing the absolute, swallowing darkness of the shaft. Hot, stale air rushed out, smelling of ancient ozone, friction, and the deep, dead earth.

"Behold!" the Priest screamed, throwing his arms wide. "The Bounty!"

The platform rose from the dark. It was a massive slab of steel, scarred by centuries of use, capable of carrying a tank regiment.

It was empty.

Kara felt her stomach drop. No! Not empty.

In the center of the massive platform, sitting alone in the spotlight of the bay's arc lamps, was a single wooden crate.

It looked small. It looked pathetic. It sat there like an insult.

The silence in the bay was terrifying. Three thousand starving people stared at the single box. This was the reward for a month of trench warfare?

"A test!" the Priest shouted, though his voice wavered slightly, losing its theatrical edge. "The Deep Ones test our resolve! They give us only what we need, so we do not grow soft!"

He signaled the crane operator with a frantic wave. A hook descended, lifting the crate with agonizing slowness. It was set down on the inspection table in front of the pulpit.

"Overseer!" the Priest barked, pointing a gloved finger at Kara. "Verify the gift!"

Kara walked down the gantry stairs, her heavy boots clanging on the metal. She felt the eyes of the workers on her back. They weren't looking at the priest anymore; they were looking at the crate. They were hungry for food, for ammo, for a reason to keep fighting.

She approached the box. It was stamped with the geometric glyphs of the Molks. She pulled a pry-bar from her belt and cracked the seal. The wood groaned, dry and brittle. The lid popped open.

Kara looked inside. She felt a cold, hard rage settle in her chest, displacing the fear.

"Well?" the Priest demanded, leaning over the rail of his cage. "Is it Power? Is it the Holy Fire?"

Kara reached in and pulled out a rifle. It wasn't new. It was a corpse of a weapon. The barrel was warped, the metal pitted with deep rust. The stock was cracked and bound with wire. It was a weapon that had been fed into the recycling hoppers weeks ago, melted down, and reformed... badly. It was slag reshaped into the memory of a gun.

"Reforged Class-C," Kara announced, her voice flat, carrying over the silent crowd. "Defective. The casting is porous. It will blow the bolt on the first shot."

She looked into the crate. Beneath the rifles were packs of nutrient paste. She picked one up. It was light. Dried out. "Expired rations," she said. "Desiccated."

A moan went through the crowd. It wasn't anger yet; it was heartbreak. It was the sound of a faith breaking under the weight of reality.

"It is enough!" the Priest insisted, his voice rising to a panic. He scrambled down from his cage, grabbing the rifle from her. He held it up like a holy relic. "With faith, this steel will strike true! The Hinds are weak! We do not need new weapons; we need new resolve!"

Kara looked at the Priest. He was soft. His robes were clean under the grease. He didn't eat the nutrient paste; he ate the officers' rations imported from the hydroponic gardens in the Apex Spire.

"It's trash," Kara whispered to him, her voice low and dangerous. "They sent us our own garbage back."

"Silence," the Priest hissed, leaning down so only she could hear. His breath smelled of expensive synthetic wine. "Do you want a riot, Overseer? Tell them it is a blessing. Or I will have you thrown into the hopper to sweeten the next batch. The machine needs meat if it won't give metal."

Kara looked at the crowd. She saw Jonas, his eyes wide with a different kind of fear. He had the look of someone who had just realized the "song" in his head was the sound of a dying machine. If she told them the truth, that the factory was broken, that the gods were dead, they would break.

And if they broke, the Hinds would roll over them by morning.

She took the rifle back. It felt heavy and useless in her hands.

"It is... hardened," Kara lied, her voice projecting to the crowd. "Tempered in the deep fires. It will kill Hinds."

The crowd cheered. It was a weak, ragged sound. A cheer born of necessity rather than joy. But it was enough to keep them moving. The Priest smiled beneath his mask. "Distribute the bounty! Double shifts for all!"

Kara turned away, signaling her logistics team to move the crate. She walked back to Jonas, her hands shaking with suppressed rage.

"It's junk," Jonas whispered as she passed. The pain in his head was receding, leaving only a hollow, ringing silence. "Isn't it? The machine... it sounded tired, Kara. It sounded hungry."

"It's worse than junk," Kara said, watching the elevator platform descend back into the dark. "It's a receipt. The system is on standby, Jonas. It's barely running."

She looked at her manifest. She crossed out 500 Crates and wrote 1.

"We have ammo for three days," Kara said quietly. "If the Hinds attack this week... we'll be throwing rocks."

"What do we do?"

Kara looked up at the Apex Spire, where the High Pontiff lived in the clouds, far above the smog and the starving workers. "We ration," she said. "We starve. And we pray that something wakes that machine up before the Hinds figure out we're empty."

Deep below them, the earth rumbled again. It wasn't a delivery. It was a hiccup. The great engine of the war was dying, and it was taking them all with it.

Chapter Nine

The Iron Harvest

THE TUNNEL DIDN'T END. It widened, opening like a jaw unhinging to swallow them whole. For an hour, the rhythmic thrumming of the "heartbeat" had grown louder, vibrating through the soles of their boots until Elian felt it in the roots of his teeth. It wasn't just a sound; it was a physical weight, a subsonic frequency that bypassed the ears and resonated directly in the chest cavity.

Then, the smooth cylindrical walls of the corridor fell away, opening into a space so vast that the beams of their shoulder-lights were swallowed by the dark before they could find a ceiling.

"Atmosphere change," Aphra whispered, checking her wrist console. The screen flickered with jagged lines of static, struggling to interpret the sudden surge of data. "Ozone. Hydraulic fluid. And... fresh grease. It's starting."

They stood on a gantry of black iron, overlooking a cavern that stretched for miles. Below them lay a city that was not built for life, but for the industry of death.

Massive robotic arms hung from the darkness above like dead spiders. Some were beginning to twitch, their joints shrieking with the sound of metal-on-metal as the energy from the Skiff's crash filtered down into their processors. Smelting vats that had been cold for centuries now pulsed with a dull, subterranean heat, casting long, rhythmic shadows across the floor.

It was a factory in the midst of a violent, stuttering reboot.

"This is the Molk capital?" Marston asked, his voice hushed. He gripped his rifle tight. The silence of the deep pressed on him, heavy as the stone around them.

"No," Elian said, staring down at the assembly lines. He watched a cascade of jagged metal shards, the offerings from the Scavengers miles above, fall from a high chute into a smelting pit. "It's a stomach. A digestive system."

He climbed down the service ladder to the factory floor, the metal rungs vibrating with the machine's slow awakening. Aphra and Marston followed, their boots clanging in the vast, echoing space.

"The Scavengers feed the throat in the Market," Elian explained, pointing to the crucible where rusted scrap was dissolving into liquid fire. "That's the intake. This sector is for the recycling of the surface. It digests the dead history of the war to build new violence. But it's only the first layer."

They moved down a central aisle flanked by two parallel conveyor belts. The machinery was sluggish, lurching as it tried to clear centuries of dust.

On the left belt, massive hydraulic presses were stamping out curved plates of dull, pitted iron. Elian recognized the shape immediately: the breastplates of the Hind Heavy Infantry. On the right belt, dipping mechanisms were lowering intricate frames into chemical baths, emerging with the distinct yellow tint of the Horn gas masks.

"They are made together," Elian whispered, tracing the line of the belts. "The armor that protects me and the mask that protects the man trying to kill me... they are born on the same rack."

He stopped at a sorting bay where a mountain of twisted metal sat beneath a rejection chute. He picked up a rifle barrel. It was warped, the metal porous and brittle.

"Reforged Class-C," Elian said. "This is all the factory could manage while it was starving. Re-melting the same garbage over and over. But look at the seismic readings."

He pointed to a set of massive drills further down the line, rooted into the bedrock. They weren't turning yet, but they were humming with a deep, hungry resonance.

"Now that the energy is back, the factory is reaching deeper," Aphra noted, her eyes scanning the dark horizon of the cavern. "Those are mining rigs. Once the startup is complete, it won't need the scrap from the surface anymore. It will mine raw materials from the mantle. It won't just re-forge the war; it will create it brand new."

As if to prove her point, they found a single pallet sitting apart from the piles of recycled junk. It sat beneath a high-speed assembly unit that was just beginning to glow with a clean, blue light.

Elian pried the lid off the nearest crate. Inside, nestled in pristine foam, were rifles unlike anything he had seen in the Hind armory. They were sleek, heavy, and black, their surfaces catching the light and swallowing it.

"MK-IV Pulse Rifles," Marston breathed, reaching for one. "These aren't Class-C. These are... perfect."

Elian ran a hand over the cold metal, feeling a sudden chill. "In the restricted archives, there were accounts of the 'First Shift'. Arms that never failed, steel that never rusted. I thought it was just myth, a story we told to make our own rot feel like a temporary failure."

"It wasn't a myth," Aphra said, her gaze fixed on the rising energy signatures on her console. "The sensors are picking up heavy seismic activity from the lower mantles. The energy we brought has kickstarted the extraction protocols. It's stopped scavenging the surface, Elian. It's starting to dig."

"The inventory is low," Kaelen murmured from behind them.

The pilot was standing by a control console, his skin looking grey in the blue light, the veins in his neck pulsing black. He wasn't looking at the crates; he was staring at the floor, as if he could see the energy flowing through the copper veins beneath the stone.

"The System is anxious," Kaelen whispered. "It wants to meet the quota. The shift is starting, and we're standing on the intake."

High above them, a hydraulic hiss cut through the silence. One of the spider-like arms twitched with sudden, fluid grace. From the ventilation grates on the cavern walls, a black, viscous fluid began to drip. It didn't splash; it coalesced.

"Shadows," Elian yelled, backing away.

The substance pooled and rose, forming three jagged, flickering silhouettes. The Supervisors. They stood between the group and the tunnel exit, their forms vibrating with a low, hungry hum. The temperature in the cavern plummeted, breath misting in the sudden cold as the factory's reboot accelerated.

"Fire!" Aphra ordered.

Marston opened up with his Recon rifle, the energy bolts passing through the Shadows as if they were smoke. The entities didn't flinch; they slid forward, moving in the spaces between seconds.

"Run!" Elian pointed deeper into the factory, toward a magnetic rail line where a flatbed transport sled was locked into a docking clamp. "To the transit line!"

They sprinted through the maze of assembly belts. Behind them, the factory was roaring to life. Lights were flickering on for miles, illuminating a landscape of silent sentinels and screaming machines. The "stomach" was full, and the machine was finally ready to eat.

"Get on the sled!" Elian scrambled onto the metal platform, dragging Kaelen with him.

The Shadows were closing in, but as Kaelen slammed his hand onto the sled's glowing console, his black veins flared in sync with the machine.

CLANG.

The docking clamps released. The sled jerked forward, accelerating into the black tunnel ahead, leaving the stuttering factory behind as it began its long, violent journey toward full capacity.

Chapter Ten

The Hunger of the Deep

THE DARK WAS NOT EMPTY. It was a solid, rushing weight that they punched through at a velocity that turned the tunnel walls into a lethal, screaming blur.

The transport sled hummed, a smooth, frictionless glide that defied the rust and ruin of the world above. They were hurtling through the arterial veins of the planet, sitting atop crates of munitions destined for a war that hadn't seen such craftsmanship in centuries. The wind of their passage tore at their clothes, stripping the heat from their bodies despite the deep, dry warmth of the tunnel.

Elian gripped the edge of the flatbed, his knuckles white. Every time he closed his eyes, he saw the afterimage of the factory floor, the spider-like arms, the molten metal, the digestive "stomach" of the world.

Beside him, Aphra was checking the power cell on Marston's rifle. Her movements were mechanical, a way to keep her hands from shaking. Her face was grey, smeared with the soot of the factory and the ash of her own shattered assumptions.

"They didn't bleed," Aphra said, her voice barely audible over the magnetic whine. She wasn't talking to anyone in particular. "Marston shot them point-blank. No debris. No biological residue. Just... dissipation."

"It's not smoke," Marston muttered. He was staring back into the blackness of the tunnel, his eyes wide and unblinking. He was the last guard, and the weight of that solitude was pressing on him. "Davis... I saw him. In the smoke. It didn't just kill him. It drank him."

Marston surged his rifle up, aiming at the empty tunnel behind them. "Back off!"

"Marston!" Aphra lunged, grabbing the barrel of his rifle and forcing it down. "There's nothing there. Save the charge. We can't afford to waste a single shot."

"They're following the heat trail," Marston hissed, his eyes darting. "Like leeches. They can smell the capacitors in our suits."

"Not leeches." Kaelen spoke from the center of the sled.

The pilot was curled against a crate of pulse rifles. He wasn't shivering anymore. He looked strangely calm, his eyes fixed on the blur of the tunnel walls as if reading a text scrolling at high speed. The black veins on his neck had spread, webbing up his jawline like frostbite made of ink. Where his skin touched the metal of the sled, the steel seemed to ripple, as if reacting to a magnetic pull.

"They are biology," Kaelen said softly. "Just... stripped. Distilled."

Elian crawled over the swaying platform to sit near him, putting himself between the pilot and the unstable guard. "What do you mean, stripped?"

Kaelen tapped his temple. "When I was connected... when the Skiff went down... I felt them pull. They didn't just drain the battery, Elian. They tasted it. It was the first time they've eaten real food in centuries."

He looked at Aphra, his pupils vibrating. "You call them Shadows. But the System remembers them as... Custodians. Flesh and bone, once. A long time ago."

"The Molks?" Elian asked.

"No. Something the Molks made? Or maybe something that adapted to the Molks' machines." Kaelen closed his eyes, tilting his head as if listening to a frequency only he could hear. "Imagine living in the dark for seven hundred years. Imagine the radiation, the chemical runoff, the gravity leaks. Flesh fails. Bone rots. So they evolved. They shed the heavy parts. They became... efficient."

Aphra stared at him, horrified. "You're saying they evolved into pure energy?"

"Not energy," Kaelen corrected. "Hunger. They are formless because form requires maintenance. They are just nervous systems and appetites now."

He pointed upward, toward the crushing weight of rock and the surface miles above.

"They hunt up there. We saw them in the Market, Elian. The Supervisors. They drift through the Grey Zone, looking for heat, for electricity, for life. They drink it, and they bring it down here. They are the spark plugs. The starters. They feed on the surface and discharge into the control systems. That's how the machines keep running while the deep mines are silent."

Elian looked at the humming rails beneath the sled. The realization hit him like a physical blow. "The war... the Seven Hundred Year War. It's not just a stalemate, is it?"

"It's a harvest," Aphra whispered, her voice hollow. "The constant fighting, the explosions, the energy expenditure... it's all just a way to keep the battery charged."

"Until today," Kaelen said, his voice flat. "The energy we brought was high-yield. High-calorie. You didn't just crash, Sub-Director. You were the ignition key. The factory isn't running on the Shadows' scraps anymore. It's reached the mantle. It's feeding on the planet's core."

Aphra slumped, the fight draining out of her. She looked at her hands. The sleek, silver material of her gloves suddenly looked less like armor and more like the flint that had struck the steel.

"Deceleration!" Marston yelled, grabbing the rail.

The whine of the sled changed pitch, dropping from a scream to a heavy, industrial thrum. The darkness ahead broke.

They burst into a space so large it defied description. It was a cavern the size of a city, lit by the dull red glow of thousands of warning lights. This was the Transit Hub. It was a kaleidoscope of motion. Hundreds of magnetic tracks converged here from the dark tunnels of the factory, weaving over and under each other like a basket made of steel.

Sleds were everywhere. Some were carrying raw ingots. Some were carrying chemicals. But most were carrying weapons.

"The Sorting," Elian said, pointing to a massive junction ahead. "Look."

At the junction, giant mechanical arms scanned the passing sleds. A sled carrying the iron breastplates of the Hinds was shunted to the left track, the Southern Line. A sled carrying crates of Horn gas masks was shunted to the right, the Northern Line.

"Left for Hinds. Right for Horns," Elian deciphered. "It's sorting the war."

Their sled approached the junction. A red laser scanned the barcodes on their crates.

Beep.

The track shifted with a bone-jarring clank. Their sled lurched to the right.

"We're going North," Elian realized. "We're following the masks. We're headed into Horn territory."

"The Horn Citadel," Kaelen murmured, his eyes tracking the lights. "It's built directly on top of the main exhaust port. It has the widest throat. If the system is purging inventory, it will use the biggest exit."

Elian looked at the track diverging to the South. It was busy, too. Sleds piled high with heavy shells were rushing toward the Hind lines. Both sides were being re-armed simultaneously with weapons that wouldn't jam, armor that wouldn't break.

The machine was no longer stuttering. It was waking up, and it was hungry for a bigger war.

"We have to get to the surface," Elian said, turning his back on the Southern Line. He looked ahead, into the dark tunnel where the Northern Line disappeared. "If we're going to the Horn Citadel, we're walking into the heart of the fire. We need to be ready to run the moment this thing stops."

The sled picked up speed again, leaving the hub behind. They were no longer just survivors; they were a delivery. And the address was Hell.

Chapter Eleven

The Mirror in the Smoke

THE MOUNTAIN'S THROAT swallowed the track, hauling them from the sterile dark of the deep earth toward the suffocating reality of the surface.

When the transport sled hit the sudden incline, the magnetic drive whined, straining against gravity. The recycled atmosphere of the Molk tunnels vanished, replaced instantly by a draft that tasted of sulfur, unwashed bodies, and chemical fire.

"Masks up," Aphra ordered, her voice tight. She pulled her rebreather over her face, the seals hissing as they locked. "Atmospheric scrubbers to maximum. The air in the Horn Citadel is thirty percent industrial runoff. It's not oxygen; it's exhaust."

Elian didn't have a helmet. He pulled his scarf, still stained with the black ink of his old life, over his nose and mouth. The smog stung his eyes, turning the world into a hazy, bruised orange. He looked at the walls of the shaft. They were no longer the seamless stone of the Ancients; they were scarred with centuries of crude repairs, welded iron patches, and prayers scratched into the soot.

"We're breaching," Kaelen whispered. He was huddled against the crates, his hands clamped over his ears. "So much noise. They scream so much up here. They are praying to the pipes, but the pipes don't listen."

The sled crested the ramp and leveled out. The darkness of the tunnel exploded into light. Not sunlight, but the harsh, sputtering glare of sodium-arc lamps hanging in the smog like dying stars. They had arrived, but not to a welcome. They had arrived to a panic.

The Receiving Bay of the Horn Citadel was a cathedral of rust. It was a cavernous space, hollowed out of the mountain not by precision lasers, but by centuries of pickaxes and desperation. Massive chains hung from the ceiling like iron votives, dripping with grease that pooled on the floor in iridescent slicks. Steam vented from cracked pipes, obscuring the far walls in a permanent, toxic fog that tasted of copper and fanaticism.

Everywhere, there were people. But they weren't standing in their usual prayer circles; they were scrambling. The blast doors had barely opened in time to admit the sled, the ancient gears screaming in protest at being forced awake so soon after the last shift. The mountain never spoke twice in one week. The last delivery had been a single crate of refuse, a cruel test of faith that had left the air thick with disappointment. This sudden, violent return felt less like a gift and more like a judgment.

"Get down," Elian hissed, dragging Aphra behind a stack of ammo crates.

They peered through the gaps in the boxes. The floor of the bay was swarming. Thousands of figures in heavy, rubberized trench coats stained a sickly yellow stood in concentric circles. On their backs, they carried twin air tanks feeding into masks with dual vertical filters that jutted from their faces like tusks.

"The Horns," Marston whispered, sighting down his rifle. His hand shook slightly; the sheer number of enemies was overwhelming. "Target-rich environment. We won't last ten seconds."

"Hold fire," Aphra commanded, placing a hand on the barrel. Her eyes scanned the crowd, not looking for threats, but for logic. "Look at them. They aren't patrolling. They're terrified. They don't know what this is."

Elian squinted through the smoke. The Horn soldiers weren't moving toward the sled with reverence; they were approaching it with the caution of men nearing a bomb. The platform beneath the sled was scarred by centuries of scarcity, the iron worn smooth by the landing of empty cages and the shuffling feet of starving shifts. But now, that history was obliterated by the sheer weight of the present. They were looking at a mountain of fresh, gleaming black rifles, crates of pristine ammunition, and power cells that hummed with full charges. It was too much, too soon.

To the starving eyes of the faithful, this was no mere logistical transfer. It was a metallic Rapture descending to lift them from the ash.

A figure in red robes, filthy, patched with tape, but distinctly ceremonial, stepped forward. He raised a staff topped with a rusted cog.

"The Deep Ones provide!" the priest bellowed, his voice distorted by amplifiers that cracked with static. Even his voice held a tremor of uncertainty. He looked at the overflow of weapons as if expecting them to vanish into the fog.

"The Deep Ones provide!" the soldiers chanted back, a ragged chorus of hunger and awe. They surged forward, driven by a desperation that overrode their fear. Hands reached out, caressing the cold steel of the crates as if it were the flesh of a saint.

"They think it's a gift," Elian realized, his stomach churning. "They don't know it's an automated backlog triggered by a glitch. They think their god finally woke up."

"It's pathetic," Aphra whispered, though her voice held more pity than contempt. "They're starving, Elian. Look at the way they move. They're worshipping a vending machine because it's the only thing that feeds them."

The priest walked up to the sled, running a gloved hand lovingly over the rifles. He was weeping. "Fresh steel," he intoned, his voice trembling with genuine ecstasy. "Born from the Womb of the World. Take it! Take it and purify the unbelievers! The drought is over!"

The bay erupted. Laborers rushed forward, struggling under the weight of the crates. They weren't super-soldiers; up close, Elian saw that their coats were patched and their eyes were yellowed by sulfur exposure.

"They're starving," Elian whispered. "Just like the Hinds. We starve for the Doctrine of Continuity; they starve for the Gifts of the Deep. It's the same lie, Aphra. Just a different dialect."

"We need to move," Aphra said, scanning the bay. "Before they unload our crate and find the passengers."

"Where?" Marston asked. "There's no cover. Just bodies."

"The steam." Elian pointed to a massive vent expelling thick white clouds near the north wall. "If we can reach the maintenance gantries, we can climb into the upper city. I know the layout of typical Horn industrial zones. The command spires are always built on the exhaust stacks to keep the heat."

They moved as one, crouching low, using the chaotic bustle of the unloading crews as cover. They slipped from the sled to a pile of scrap metal, then to the shadow of a crane. Behind them, the shaft rumbled again. A second sled burst from the darkness, piled high with heavy ordnance. Then a third. The inventory wasn't stopping. The "miracle" was turning into an avalanche.

They were ten feet from the steam vent when Kaelen stopped.

He didn't freeze in fear; he froze in recognition. He stood up, fully exposed, staring at a young Horn soldier who had removed his mask to wipe sweat from his face. The soldier was no older than twenty, his skin pockmarked with chemical burns.

"He hears it too," Kaelen said loudly. "The hum. He has the ear."

The soldier froze. He looked up and saw Kaelen, a man in a shimmering, impossible silver suit standing amidst the grime. But it wasn't the suit the soldier looked at. It was Kaelen's face. The black veins pulsing under his translucent skin matched the rhythm of the mountain. His eyes were voids of liquid darkness. He didn't look human; he looked like the machine made flesh.

Kaelen reached out a hand. It wasn't a threat. It was an invitation.

For a second, nobody moved. The soldier didn't raise his rifle. He dropped it. The weapon clattered on the deck, forgotten. He fell to his knees, staring at Kaelen with terrifying devotion.

"Angel?" the soldier whispered, tears cutting tracks through the soot on his face.

"Movement!" a voice roared from the gantry above. "Intruders on the deck!"

A siren began to wail. It was a mechanical scream that tore through the smoke.

"Go!" Aphra shouted. She shoved Kaelen toward the roar of the north wall, breaking the connection. They plunged into the white plume of the exhaust vent. The heat was an immediate, physical blow, turning the sweat inside Elian's suit into a boiling film. He fumbled for a rusted ladder, his fingers slipping on rungs coated in a century of condensed grease. Above them, the vent howled like a gale-force wind, the pressure of the mountain's breath nearly pushing them off the iron.

Elian hauled himself upward, his muscles screaming. The world below, the screaming priest, the clattering rifles, and the kneeling boy, dissolved into a featureless white blur. The transition was abrupt. One moment they were in the vaulted, echoing scale of the cathedral-bay; the next, they were squeezed into the "Lungs" of the Citadel.

It was a vertical labyrinth of bypass valves and cooling fins where the air didn't just smell of sulfur; it felt like a solid weight in the chest. They climbed between two massive, throbbing conduits that radiated a dry, blistering heat, the space so narrow that their packs scraped against the vibrating metal.

"Don't stop!" Aphra's voice was a ragged command from somewhere below him in the mist. "Keep climbing! If the pressure spikes, this shaft becomes a furnace!"

Elian reached a metal catwalk, his lungs burning as he hauled himself out of the primary draft. He collapsed onto the grating, coughing violently as the others tumbled up behind him.

Below them, the blast doors of the shaft didn't close. Sled after sled slammed into the docking cradle, crushing the ones before them. The mountain was vomiting its hoard, and the sound of the metal-on-metal violence echoed up through the pipes like the heartbeat of a dying god.

"They're blocking the lower exits!" Marston reported, checking the thermal feed on his rifle. "We're being herded up."

"Up is where we want to go," Elian wheezed, wiping soot from his eyes. "The Command Center will be at the peak. If we want to stop this, we have to go to the top."

He looked down through the grate one last time. The Horn soldier, the boy who had seen Kaelen, was still on his knees, ignoring the chaos, praying to the spot where the "Angel" had stood. He was smiling, serene amidst the disaster.

"They aren't the enemy," Elian said, mostly to himself. "They're just the other half of the battery."

"They will shoot us regardless," Aphra said, reloading her weapon. "Move, Vost. We're in the belly of the beast now."

They ran into the dark industrial maze of the Citadel, leaving the worship of the guns behind them, climbing toward the people who pulled the trigger.

Chapter Twelve

The High Altar of Lies

THE ASCENT WAS A JOURNEY through the layers of a dying lung. They climbed for an hour, hauling themselves up vertical maintenance ladders that slicked their hands with oil and condensation. With every rung, the atmosphere changed texture, but never for the better. At the bottom, it was thick with the wet, heavy congestion of the Receiving Bay, oil smoke and unwashed bodies. As they passed the mid-levels, the draft turned dry and wheezing, filled with the acrid dust of the ore crushers. By the time they reached the upper gantries, the air was thin and sharp, stinging with the chemical ozone of high-altitude filters that hadn't been serviced in a decade.

The ascent should have been impossible. They were invading the heart of the enemy stronghold, yet they met no resistance.

They passed Level 40, the Garrison Deck. It should have been a choke point, swarming with internal security. Instead, the blast doors were locked open, and the corridors were silent. Abandoned meals sat on guard tables, the steam still rising from bowls of gruel. Weapons racks stood stripped bare.

"Where are they?" Marston whispered, his rifle tracking empty air. His nerves were fraying in the silence. "This feels like a trap."

"It's not a trap," Aphra said, looking down through the floor grate at the distant, reddish glow of the bay miles below. "It's a migration. The guards didn't mobilize to stop us; they mobilized to see the miracle. They went down to the Rapture."

Elian led the way, his map-maker's eyes finding patterns in the chaos. But even the automated defenses seemed complicit. At the junction of the Ventilation Spire, a ceiling-mounted turret swiveled toward them, its tracking laser painting a red dot on Aphra's chest.

Marston froze. "Contact!"

The turret whirred, the barrels spinning up with the hungry whine of capacitors charging. The targeting laser cut through the gloom, slashing away from Aphra to snap onto Kaelen. It lingered there, tracing the grey topography of his skin and the black, pulsing tributaries of his veins with cold precision.

For a heartbeat, the machine hesitated, caught in a logic loop between target and command. Then, the whine died. The laser winked out. The turret didn't just retract; it slumped back into its housing with a sound like a heavy exhale.

"It doesn't see a target," Kaelen murmured, his voice sounding like dry leaves skittering on stone. "It sees a signature. I am not an intruder to this machine. I am a command code written in flesh."

"It's not a sentry," Aphra breathed, the realization hitting her with the force of a physical blow. She reached out, hovering her hand over the cooling barrel to read the heat signature. "Look at the targeting logic. It prioritizes biological containment, not tactical defense. It wasn't guarding the stairs from intruders, Elian. It was a seal. It was designed to keep the factory floor quarantined from the command deck."

"And I just unlocked the gate," Kaelen whispered, staring into the dark shaft below where the shadows seemed to be stretching upward. "The quarantine is lifted. The doors I open... they don't close behind me."

The Citadel was a fortress built to repel armies, but against the architecture of its own masters, it was defenseless. It was an organism that had finally forgotten how to distinguish between its own blood and the poison killing it.

The journey continued, but the silence had changed texture; it was no longer empty, it was complicit. Every rung was a battle against gravity and exhaustion. Aphra covered the rear, her breath hitching with the pain of bruised ribs, her rifle tracking the shadows that seemed to pool in the corners of the shaft. Between them, Marston half-carried Kaelen. The pilot was dead weight, his boots scraping against the metal rungs.

Kaelen was changing.

In the tunnels, he had been a conduit, frightened, but useful. Now, severed from the immediate proximity of the Deep Roads, he was unraveling. He wasn't shivering from cold anymore; he was shaking from a withdrawal that went down to his marrow.

"It's too quiet," Kaelen gasped as they paused on a grated landing to catch their breath. He clawed at the collar of his suit, his fingernails leaving white streaks on the synthetic skin. "The song... it's fading. I can't hear the heartbeat."

"That's a good thing, Kaelen," Elian said gently, offering him water from the flask. "We're away from the Shadows. We're climbing out of the machine."

Kaelen slapped the flask away. His eyes were wide, the pupils blown so large that his irises were thin rings of blue swimming in black oil. "No! You don't understand. The silence... it isn't empty. It's heavy. It presses in like water. It feels like... amputation."

He looked at his hands. The veins beneath the skin weren't blue anymore. They were darkening, turning the color of the necrotic soil in the No Man's Land, pulsing with a slow, thick rhythm that didn't match his heart.

"I need to go back," Kaelen whispered, his voice cracking. "I'm not finished. They started... knitting me. I'm undone."

Aphra grabbed his chin, forcing him to look at her. "You are human, Kaelen. You stay with us. We are going to the top, and then we are getting out of this madness. Focus."

Kaelen nodded, but his gaze drifted past her, toward the deep earth miles below. He wasn't just a pilot anymore; he was a bridge that had been burned at one end, the smoke still rising from his soul.

They breached the upper levels through a service hatch behind a massive air filtration unit. The transition was jarring. One moment, they were in the grime and noise of the industrial sector, surrounded by the smell of burning ozone and sweat; the next, they were standing on a carpet of deep, plush crimson.

The air here was cool, scrubbed clean of sulfur and rot. It smelled of lavender and polished wood. The walls were not rusted steel, but mahogany inlaid with gold leaf. Silence reigned here. Not the silence of the void, but the silence of insulation. The screams of the dying city below were filtered out, reduced to a polite hum.

"We made it," Elian whispered, wiping a smear of grease from his cheek. "The Command Deck." He looked at his dirty boots on the pristine carpet. "It looks like a palace."

"It is a palace," Aphra said with disgust, checking the charge on her rifle. "While their people wear rags and breathe poison, the leadership lives in a humidor."

Marston spat on the floor. "Starving workers in the basement, gold leaf in the attic. Doesn't matter what planet you're on, the view from the top is always the same."

They moved silently down the corridor. There were no guards here; the enemy was miles away across the No Man's Land, and the faithful were miles below in the smog. The Horn leadership felt safe in their tower, protected by altitude and arrogance. At the end of the hall stood double doors of heavy oak, carved with gear-and-tusk motifs inlaid with real ivory.

"Breaching charge," Aphra signaled.

Marston placed a small magnetic disc on the lock. *Thump.* The doors blew inward with a dull concussive cough, splinters raining into the room beyond. They stormed the room, weapons raised.

It was a war room, but it looked more like a banquet hall. A long table dominated the space, laden with real food. Bowls of fruit that had never seen the smog. Roasted meats that dripped fat. Crystal decanters of wine. The holographic map of the Frontline flickered in the center, ignored.

Around the table sat five men. They didn't wear gas masks; they wore silk robes. They were healthy, well-fed, and currently frozen in shock, wine goblets halfway to their mouths. At the head of the table sat a man who didn't look shocked. He looked annoyed. He was older, his hair a mane of silver, his face lined with the easy authority of someone who has never been told 'no'. He wore the red vestments of the High Priesthood, but they were tailored, clean, and expensive.

"High Pontiff Varus," Elian said, recognizing the face from the propaganda leaflets dropped over the trenches. "The Voice of the Deep."

Varus set his wine down slowly. He looked at the dirty, desperate group invading his sanctuary, his eyes lingering on Aphra's silver suit. He didn't see enemies; he saw interruptions.

"And you must be the 'Angels' my floor managers are screaming about," Varus said. His voice was smooth, a rich baritone trained for sermons. "You're late. I expected you to be captured in the Receiving Bay."

"Get on the ground!" Marston shouted, his finger trembling on the trigger. He wanted to shoot.

Varus waved a hand dismissively. "Oh, put those away. If you were going to kill me, you would have bombed the tower. You walked up here. That means you want something. Information? Leverage? A ride home?"

Aphra stepped forward, kicking a chair aside. Her anger was cold and sharp. "We want to know why you are feeding your people into a meat grinder."

"A meat grinder?" Varus turned his gaze to her. He didn't blink. "You have a lot of moral authority for a stranger. You aren't Horn. And you certainly aren't Hind. You smell like ozone, not cabbage."

He leaned back, his eyes tracing the lines of her silver suit.

"You are the 'Newness' my scouts whispered about before the comms died. The visitor from the West." He gestured to Elian. "And yet, you travel with a Hind. You landed your silver ship in their courtyard, not mine. You chose your side before you even opened the hatch."

"We didn't choose a side," Aphra snapped, though her grip on her rifle tightened. "We came as surveyors. We came to map the conflict."

"Surveyors?" Varus laughed, a harsh, barking sound. "Surveyors measure the land, Angel. Soldiers breach doors. You didn't come to map the war; you came to join it. You just picked the side with the bigger tanks."

"He isn't starving his own people," Aphra countered.

"Isn't he?" Varus asked softly. "Look south, girl. General Korm feeds his legions to the mud for the 'Doctrine of Continuity.' I feed mine to the machine for 'The Bounty.' We are doing the exact same thing. The only difference is the prayer we recite while we do it."

He spread his hands. "We are just two shopkeepers haggling over the price of breath. Don't pretend your hands are clean just because your suit is shiny."

"It's a lie," Elian spat, stepping up to the table. He slammed his hand down on the polished wood, leaving a bloody handprint next to the fruit bowl. "It's not about the politics, Varus. It's about the source. We saw the factory. We saw the delivery line. You know the weapons aren't miracles. You know they come from the Molks. You aren't receiving gifts from gods; you're scavenging from a grave."

Varus's smile vanished. He leaned forward, his eyes hard and cynical.

"Of course I know," he snapped. "Do you take me for a fool? I know exactly where the rifles come from. I know about the tunnels. I know about the Shadows."

"Then why?" Aphra asked. "Why maintain the charade? You could stop the war. You could use the tunnels to negotiate peace."

"Peace?" Varus scoffed. "And do what? Look at the land out there. It's dead. The soil is poison. The water is acid. We have no agriculture. We have no industry. We have nothing but the war."

He stood up, his robes rustling like dry paper.

"The war is our economy. The 'miracles', the guns, the ammo, they are the only resource we have. If I tell my people that their gods are just automated machines, the society collapses. Despair kills them faster than bullets." He pointed a manicured finger at Elian. "I don't feed them to the grinder because I hate them. I feed them because the grinder produces the only thing that keeps us alive: Purpose. And supplies. Without me to bless the crates, they are just starving animals in a cage. I give them a reason to endure the smog."

"You give them death," Elian said. "You trade their lives for comfort."

"I trade their lives for order," Varus corrected. "And order is expensive."

"You're a parasite," Kaelen spoke up.

The pilot stepped out from behind Marston. He looked wretched, sweating, pale, his veins pulsing with that dark, unnatural color. But his voice was terrifyingly resonant. It sounded like the wind rushing through a deep tunnel.

"The System doesn't care about your economy," Kaelen rasped. "The System is waking up. And it considers you... obsolete. A redundant component."

Varus looked at Kaelen, and for the first time, the Pontiff looked unsettled. He saw the hybrid nature of the pilot. He saw the way the shadows seemed to cling to him even in the bright room.

"What are you?" Varus whispered.

"I am the new connection," Kaelen said, his eyes rolling back. "And the line is busy."

Before Varus could respond, the holographic map in the center of the table turned red. A siren, the real air-raid siren, began to wail across the entire city. It was a sound of doom.

"What did you do?" Varus demanded, looking at his console.

"We didn't do anything," Aphra said, checking her wrist readout. "Massive energy spike detected. From below. Directly below us."

Kaelen collapsed to his knees, clutching his head.

"They're coming," Kaelen screamed. "They followed us up! The hunger is here!"

The floor of the opulent war room shook. Deep in the bowels of the mountain, the delivery shaft they had ridden up was no longer just delivering crates. The holy barriers of the Citadel were never meant to stop the dark from rising from the throat of the world itself.

Chapter Thirteen

The Light That Burns

THE FLOOR OF THE SPIRE didn't just shake; it groaned. It was a low resonant frequency, the sound of stone grinding against stone, of a mountain trying to digest a meal too large for its stomach.

High Pontiff Varus stumbled back from the table, his wine goblet shattering on the polished floor. The red stain spread across the map of the Frontline, blotting out the tactical stalemate with a chaotic mess. The cynicism that had armored him a moment ago was stripped away, leaving only the raw, sputtering panic of a man watching his controlled ecosystem collapse.

"This is impossible," Varus stammered, his voice losing its polished baritone and cracking into a high whine. "The Sodium Perimeter... the Sanctified Fog... they burn the Shadows! They cannot cross the city limits!"

Elian stared at the Pontiff, the tactical mystery of a century resolving in a single, terrifying second. The blinding lights of the Horns weren't religious pageantry; they were a containment field.

"They didn't cross the limits, Pontiff!" Elian shouted over the rising wail of the sirens. He grabbed the edge of the table to steady himself as the room listed five degrees to the left. "They didn't walk through the front door. We brought them up from the deep. You built your palace on top of the chimney, Varus, and now the fire is coming up."

"The delivery shaft." Aphra realized, checking the energy readings on her wrist. The numbers were scrolling too fast to read. "The shielding on the shaft was designed to contain radiation, not entities. It's a highway straight past your defenses."

Kaelen was on his knees, his hands pressed against his ears as if trying to block out a deafening noise only he could hear. His back arched, the black veins pulsing through his suit.

"It's not just the Shadows," Kaelen gasped, his voice wet. "The line... the line is fully open. The factory isn't sending a shipment. It's clearing the inventory."

"What does that mean?" Varus demanded, grabbing the edge of his high-backed chair.

Kaelen looked up. His eyes were swimming with dark fluid, reflecting a terror that spanned centuries. "It means you aren't getting a monthly ration of rifles. You're getting seven hundred years of backlog. In ten minutes, the Receiving Bay will be crushed under the weight of the metal. The Citadel will be buried in its own miracles."

The double doors of the War Room buckled. Not from an explosion, but from a cold, heavy pressure pushing from the hallway. Frost began to spiderweb across the gold-leaf inlay, cracking the wood with sounds like pistol shots.

The men in silk didn't wait to see what was behind the wood. The facade of their authority crumbled with the first crack of the door. They scrambled for the service hatch at the back of the room, fighting each other to squeeze through as expensive robes tore on the iron latch. They vanished into the dark service corridors, leaving their wine half-drunk and their Pontiff alone at the head of the table.

"They're here," Marston yelled, leveling his rifle at the buckling doors. His face was a mask of sweat and soot. "I count... too many signatures. They're in the walls."

"We can't fight them in here," Aphra said, her tactical mind overriding her fear. She turned to Varus. "Does this tower have an evacuation route? A launch pad?"

Varus stared at the freezing door, paralyzed. He was a master of leverage, a man who had spent forty years turning starvation into piety and iron into gold. But there was no leverage here. He was watching his empire collapse, realizing with terrifying clarity that a monster cannot be bribed.

Elian stepped forward. He saw the panic in Varus's eyes. The glazing over of a mind refusing to process reality. He knew he couldn't threaten the Pontiff; fear had already paralyzed him. He had to appeal to his vanity. To his history. Elian switched languages, dropping the rough gutter-speak of the trenches to speak in the High Dialect, the archaic, formal tongue of the pre-war diplomats, a language of soft vowels and rigid hierarchy he had spent twenty years studying in the dust of the archives.

"The crown that does not move is the crown that is buried," Elian said clearly, the ancient words cutting through the noise.

Varus blinked. The familiarity of the academic phrase, the opening line of the Horn Liturgy of Succession, acted like a slap to the face. He looked at Elian with a sudden flicker of recognition.

"You speak the Old Standard," Varus whispered, straightening his spine instinctively.

"I know your history, Varus," Elian continued, keeping his voice steady, anchoring the Pontiff to the moment. "I know that the High Pontiffs keep a dirigible docked at the Apex Spire for 'inspection tours.' You can die here, clutching your wine like a peasant, or you can take us to the roof and we can try to seal the shaft from the outside."

Varus looked at the door. The wood was screaming now, splintering inward. He looked at Elian, then at Aphra's rifle. Self-preservation rewired his brain in an instant.

"The Apex," Varus spat, gathering his robes. "Access code Vermillion-Nine. But the lift is on the other side of the atrium. We have to cross the open floor."

"Then we run," Aphra said. She signaled Marston. "Formation Delta. Vost, you stick to me. If I move, you move. If I drop, you don't stop."

Elian looked at her. Her face was bruised, her suit scorched, but her eyes were clear. For the first time, he didn't see the arrogant invader who had descended from the sky to judge his world; he saw a woman who was terrified but refusing to let that terror make the decisions.

"I won't leave you behind, Aphra," Elian said quietly.

Aphra paused, surprising herself with a small, grim smile. "Then try to keep up, Cartographer."

The atrium of the Spire was a slaughterhouse of light and shadow. The emergency containment protocols had activated. Massive sodium-arc lamps, the "Holy Fire" of the Horn defenses, blasted the corridors with blinding yellow light. Where the light hit the invading Shadows, the air sizzled, smelling of ozone and burning hair.

But the Shadows were adapting. They weren't walking in the open; they were moving inside the walls, rippling through the electrical conduits and bursting out of light fixtures to drag screaming guards into the dark. The building itself had become hostile.

"Clear left!" Aphra shouted, firing a suppression burst at a vent leaking black fluid.

They sprinted across the polished marble floor. Varus ran with surprising speed, fueled entirely by the adrenaline of a rat fleeing a sinking ship.

"The lift!" Varus screamed, pointing to a gilded cage at the far end of the hall.

Between them and the lift, the floor erupted. It wasn't a Shadow. It was the factory. A massive crate, stamped with the Molk glyph for 'Heavy Ordnance', smashed up through the marble tiles, carried on a geyser of pressurized steam. The delivery system was backing up, the pressure forcing cargo through the architectural weak points of the tower.

The crate burst open on impact. Out of it poured not rifles, but machines. They were the size of dogs, spider-like, with razor limbs and glowing blue sensors. Security Drones.

"Automated defense units," Kaelen yelled, cringing away from the blue light. "The factory is sending the security detail to clear the obstruction!"

To the drones, the "obstruction" was the population of the Citadel. The machines skittered across the floor, targeting anything that moved. A squad of Horn guards near the lift was cut down in seconds, their armor useless against monofilament blades that hummed with kinetic energy.

"Elian!" Aphra tackled him as a drone leaped, its blades slicing the air where his head had been. She rolled, bringing her rifle up and blasting the machine into scrap. Sparks showered over them. She shoved Elian toward the lift. "Go! Punch the code!"

Elian scrambled to the lift panel. His hands were shaking so hard he could barely see the keys. Vermillion-Nine. He punched the keypad.

"Access Denied," the mechanical voice droned. "Security Lockdown in effect."

"Varus!" Elian shouted. "It's locked!"

Varus cowered behind a statue of a Saint holding a gear. "Override it! I don't have the override! The system has locked me out!"

"Step aside." Aphra was there. She didn't use a code. She pulled a data-spike from her wrist gauntlet. A wicked shard of silver metal. She jammed it into the panel. "This will fry the localized logic gates. It's messy. It's exactly the kind of unrefined hacking I would have fired a cadet for."

"I like the new you," Elian muttered, watching Marston hold back a wave of drones with disciplined, desperate bursts of fire.

The lift doors hissed open. "Inside!"

They piled in. Marston fired one last shot, blowing a drone out of the air, and jumped in backward. Aphra yanked the spike out, and the doors slammed shut just as a drone collided with the brass grating, its limbs scrabbling against the metal, trying to pry the cage open.

The lift jerked upward, ascending toward the roof. For a moment, there was silence, save for the heavy breathing of the survivors and the hum of the lift motor. Aphra leaned against the wall, sliding down until she was sitting. She looked exhausted. Her pristine silver suit was scorched and stained with oil. She looked at her hands, which were trembling.

Elian sat beside her. He offered her his water flask.

"You saved my life," Elian said.

Aphra took the flask, her hands shaking as she unscrewed the cap. "You saved mine. I would have shot the Pontiff. I wouldn't have known how to talk to him. I wouldn't have known the language of his vanity."

"We make a strange pair," Elian noted. "The Archivist and the Invader."

"The Arsonist," Aphra corrected bitterly. "I started this fire, Elian. Kaelen was right. We are the battery. Every death down there... it's on my ledger."

"You started it," Elian agreed, taking the flask back. "But maybe... maybe it needed to burn down. The Hinds, the Horns... we were rotting, Aphra. Slowly. Comfortably. At least now the rot is exposed." He looked at Varus, who was muttering prayers in the corner, clutching his vestments. "He calls them gods. You called them a resource. You were both wrong. They're just a machine. And machines have an off switch."

"The factory is miles underground," Aphra said. "We can't go back down. We barely got out."

"We don't need to go down," Elian said, looking up as the lift passed through the final cloud layer, revealing the stars, cold, indifferent, and beautiful. "We just need to cut the power cord."

The lift chimed. Apex Level.

"What do you mean?" Aphra asked, standing up.

"Kaelen said the Shadows are the power cords," Elian said, his eyes hard. "They connect the surface to the deep. If we can't stop the factory... maybe we can starve it."

The doors opened to the howling wind of the Citadel's roof. Tethered to the docking mast, swaying gently above the inferno like a lifeboat on a burning ocean, was a massive, armored dirigible. The Hand of the Deep.

And climbing up the sides of the spire, spilling over the parapets like ink rising in water, were the Shadows.

Chapter Fourteen

The Black Feast

THE HIGH SANCTUARY of the Spire had crumbled, its roof stripped of safety and laid bare as a banquet table for the swarm.

The Shadows poured over the parapets like oil flowing uphill, defying gravity with fluid, visceral grace. They lacked faces, but they possessed a terrifying sense of direction. They moved with the frenetic speed of starving things that had suddenly discovered a glut of food.

They ignored the humans. Elian, Aphra, and Marston were made of meat and chemical reactions, low-yield calories. The Shadows wanted the main course. They flowed past the survivors, wrapping themselves around the massive sodium-arc generators bolted to the tower's peak.

"They aren't attacking us!" Aphra yelled over the howling wind, dragging Varus toward the docking mast. "They're attacking the grid! They're feeding!"

As she spoke, the blinding yellow light of the Citadel, the "Holy Fire" that had kept the dark at bay for centuries, began to scream. The filaments in the massive bulbs vibrated at a frequency that tore at the eardrums. The light didn't fade naturally; it was extracted.

Elian watched in horror as the Shadows latched onto the generators. They turned translucent, their smoky forms filling with a raw, violet luminescence as they sucked the gigawatts out of the copper cabling. The arc-lamps dimmed, flickered, and shattered, the glass raining down like hail.

Gorged on the power, the Shadows pulsed, growing denser and taller. Then, heavy with their meal, they sank through the roof materials as if the stone were water, discharging that stolen power straight down into the mountain's roots. The floor shuddered. Deep below, the factory groaned in gratitude.

"The Hand!" Varus shrieked, clawing at the ladder of the dirigible. "Get us aboard! I command you! Get me off this rock!"

The Hand of the Deep was a relic of a more elegant age, a sleek, armored zeppelin built for luxury inspections of the Frontline. It was trimmed in brass and velvet, a floating parlor for men who liked to watch battles from a safe distance. But as Kaelen scrambled into the cockpit, the luxury felt like the lining of a coffin.

"Engines hot!" Kaelen shouted. He didn't touch the yoke; he placed his hands flat on the instrument panel. The black veins on his neck throbbed in sync with the turbine's whine. He wasn't piloting; he was communing. "Releasing moorings!"

The dirigible lurched upward, tearing free of the docking clamps just as the roof of the Spire collapsed inward, swallowed by the stone that had turned molten beneath it. Elian scrambled to the observation deck, looking down through the panoramic glass floor. What he saw made him grip the railing until his knuckles cracked.

The Citadel was dying.

With the lights gone, the city was lit only by the fires of the Receiving Bay. But the fire wasn't consuming the city. The city was consuming itself. The delivery shaft had ruptured. It no longer ejected crates; it vomited them. Metal shrieked against stone as the "trickle" of weapons became a geyser.

Seven hundred years of backlog. Millions of rifles, tons of ammunition, legions of automated drones. They were erupting from the base of the mountain. The sheer pressure of the inventory was cracking the Citadel's foundations. The Receiving Bay had already vanished, buried under a mountain of gleaming, useless steel.

"Look at them," Elian whispered, horrified.

In the streets below, the Horn citizens weren't fleeing the collapse; they were rushing toward it. Starving wretches climbed piles of crushing metal, trying to grab the "miracles" their gods were vomiting up.

Then the drones activated.

Thousands of blue lights flickered on amidst the steel deluge. The security units, confused by the chaos and lacking a valid Molk override, defaulted to their factory settings: Protect the Inventory. They designated the entire population of the Citadel as unauthorized personnel.

The slaughter was mechanical and efficient. The "miracles" turned on the believers. Monofilament blades spun, and the yellow trench coats turned red.

"My city..." Varus wept, slumped against the bulkhead. He held a crystal decanter of brandy, but his hand shook too hard to pour. "The inventory... the quarterly projections... we had a surplus."

Aphra stared at him. "People are dying, Varus. And you're talking about a surplus?"

"People are renewable!" Varus snapped, his voice cracking. "Labor grows back! But the infrastructure... the mechanism... that was the balance."

"The balance is gone, Varus," Aphra said, her voice hollow. She stood beside Elian, watching the destruction. "You wanted the factory to run? It's running. This is what total efficiency looks like."

The dirigible climbed higher, banking away from the rising smoke. The shockwave of a massive structural collapse, the Citadel's foundations finally giving way under the pressure of the rising inventory, buffeted the hull, rattling the fine china in the cabinets. Elian looked away from the burning spire. He couldn't watch the massacre any longer. He turned his gaze North.

Across the vast, dark expanse of the No Man's Land, past the twisted Slag Garden and the silence of the Grey Zone, he saw tiny pinpricks of light.

Flares.

"They can see it," Elian said softly.

Aphra followed his gaze. "The Hinds?"

"General Korm," Elian said. "He's standing on the ramparts of our Citadel right now. He's watching the enemy capital burn."

"He'll think we won," Aphra said. "He'll think your mission was a success. He'll think you crippled the Horns."

"He'll launch an offensive," Elian corrected, a new kind of fear settling in his chest. "He won't know about the factory. He won't know about the drones. He'll see smoke and he'll order a full-scale charge across the No Man's Land to claim the victory. He's going to march an army into a meat grinder."

Kaelen called out from the cockpit. His voice was distant, dreamy. He wasn't looking at the controls; he was staring blankly ahead, his mind connected to the copper nerves of the deep.

"The factory isn't stopping," Kaelen whispered. "I can feel it tearing. It's re-routing. The Horn output is blocked by the debris."

"So it shuts down?" Varus asked, hope flickering in his eyes.

"No." Kaelen turned. His face was a mask of sweat and dark veins, his eyes reflecting a map that no one else could see. "It's a network, Pontiff. If one exit is blocked, the System finds another. It must deliver."

Kaelen pointed North, toward the Hind lines, then his hand swept wider, encompassing the dark horizons beyond the war they knew.

"It's re-routing the inventory. It's opening the old vents in the No Man's Land. But the pressure is too high for just the Zone," Kaelen said, his voice trembling with the scale of the data flooding his mind. "It's pushing deeper. Into the Horn hinterlands. Into the forgotten sectors of the South. It is forcing open delivery shafts that haven't cycled since the First Shift. It's not just arming the dead ground, Elian; it's arming the ghosts."

Elian looked back at the distant Hind flares. Korm was about to march his army not into a victory, but into a hardware store run by ghosts.

"Turn the ship," Elian ordered.

"To where?" Aphra asked. "There's nowhere safe."

"Home," Elian said. "We have to beat Korm to the punch. We have to tell him that for seven hundred years, we were the ones choosing the targets. We were the ones managing the decay. We played at being gods because the machine was too hungry to ignore us, but too tired to replace us."

He watched a geyser of blue light erupt from a mountain range fifty miles to the West. A sector that had been silent for three centuries.

"The war isn't just a conflict anymore, Aphra," Elian whispered, the weight of the archives pressing down on him. "It's become an objective. The factory isn't waiting for our commands. It's analyzing the throughput. It's clearing the backlog by ensuring there is always something left to shoot at. We've been fired, Aphra. The war isn't over. It's just been automated."

Chapter Fifteen

The Traitor's Sky

THE HAND OF THE DEEP drifted through the smoke like a ghost ship, its engines coughing against the headwinds of the No Man's Land. The observation deck's luxury, its velvet divans and crystal decanters, felt grotesque against the backdrop of the burning horizon.

High Pontiff Varus sat on a divan bolted to the floor, staring at his hands. They were shaking. Not from fear, but with the frantic adrenaline of a gambler who has lost the entire pot and is already looking for a loan. For forty years, he had been the Voice. He had interpreted the rumbles of the mountain for millions of souls, maintaining the Lie because it was the mortar holding the bricks of society together.

Now, the bricks were dust.

"I have no flock," Varus whispered, running his thumb over the heavy silk of his sleeve. "I have no temple. The contract is void."

Elian looked up from his map table. He was trying to calculate their drift using a sextant and the few stars visible through the smog. "You're still alive, Varus. That counts for something."

"Alive?" Varus laughed, a sound like glass breaking. "A Pontiff without a god is just a madman in a costume. If the Horns find me, they will tear me apart for abandoning them. If the Hinds find me, they will execute me as a symbol." He looked up, his eyes hard and calculating. "I cannot be the High Pontiff anymore, Cartographer. That man died in the fire."

"Then who are you?" Aphra asked sharply. She stood at the window, scanning the horizon with a pair of pilfered binoculars. "We don't need a priest right now. We need someone who knows how the Horns fight. Because if we survive this landing, your people might be the ones hunting us."

Varus looked at her, then down at his red robes. The Vestments of the Gear, embroidered with gold thread worth more than a soldier's life. "My people," Varus murmured. "They died praying to a machine because I told them it was listening. They were fuel, Sub-Director. Burnt to keep the engine warm."

He stood up. He didn't look broken anymore; he looked dangerous.

"Take off the coat," Aphra said. "You're a target in that red."

Varus didn't need to be told twice. He began to unbutton the heavy brocade vest. This wasn't just undressing; it was a resignation. With every button, he dismantled the myth of the Voice.

"The Hinds hate the Pontiff," Varus said, his voice dropping to a conspiratorial whisper. "But they love intelligence. They love maps. They love leverage." He paused, his eyes locking onto Elian's with predatory sharpness. "You draw the lines, don't you, Cartographer? But lines are just geometry without secrets."

He let the heavy, gold-encrusted robe fall to the floor, treating the holy garment like a dirty rag. Beneath it, he wore a simple linen shirt, now stained with the soot of his burning city.

"I know where the ammo dumps are," Varus said, planning his own treason in real-time. "I know the cipher codes for the Horn artillery. I know which generals can be bribed and which ones are true believers. You have the parchment, Elian, but I have the legend. If you want to survive Korm, you need to bring him a map he can use to win. I am that map."

He stepped closer, invading Elian's space.

"We are partners now. I provide the secrets; you provide the credibility. You validate my intel, and I make you indispensable to your General. Without me, you are just a traitor who lost a ship. With me, you are the man who delivered the Horn Dominion on a platter. I am not a priest, Elian. I am an asset. If we meet Korm, I am not his enemy. I am his key to the North."

"You'd sell out your own culture?" Elian asked, disgusted but fascinated by the speed of the conversion.

"I have no culture," Varus said, smoothing his shirt. "I have survival. The Horns are dead. Long live the Hinds."

"Contact front!" Marston's voice cracked from the cockpit intercom.

Elian rushed to the window. Through the gloom, the Hind lines were visible. A jagged scar of concrete and barbed wire stretching across the horizon. But something was wrong. Usually, the Hind lines were dark, hiding from Horn artillery. Tonight, they were ablaze with searchlights. Massive shapes moved in the mud. Land-Crawlers the size of cathedrals, walkers with hydraulic legs, and caissons of heavy ordnance.

"They're mobilizing," Elian realized. "Korm isn't waiting for morning. He sees the fire at the Horn Citadel. He's launching the invasion now."

"They see us," Aphra warned. "We're a Horn vessel entering their airspace. We look like a bomber."

"Flash the signal!" Elian shouted to Kaelen. "Pattern Delta-Six! Friendlies inbound!"

"I'm trying!" Kaelen yelled back. "But the external lights are dead! The Shadows ate the circuits!"

On the ground miles below, a battery of flak cannons turned their muzzles skyward. To the Hinds, the dirigible was just a slow-moving target coming to spoil their victory parade.

"Brace!" Aphra screamed, grabbing a support strut.

The sky erupted. It wasn't a clean shot. The Hind flak shells were old, fused to detonate on proximity. They filled the air with jagged shrapnel, turning the sky into a blender. The Hand of the Deep didn't just explode; it disintegrated. A shell tore through the aft gondola, shearing it clean off the main hull. Elian watched in horror as the rear section, where Marston was manning the tail guns, spun away into the abyss. There was no scream over the comms, just a burst of static and a trailing arc of fire as the last guard fell into the dark.

The gas bag tore open with the long, mournful groan of escaping helium. The world tilted sideways as gravity reclaimed them. Elian was thrown against the bulkhead. He heard metal screaming, glass shattering, and the roar of the wind. They didn't fall like a stone; they spiraled, a leaf caught in a hurricane.

CRUNCH.

Darkness.

Elian woke to the smell of ozone and wet earth. He was hanging upside down, strapped into his seat. The observation deck was gone. It was sheared off upon impact. He was staring at the mossy ground three feet below his head. He fumbled with the buckle, falling into the mud with a wet thud.

"Aphra?" he croaked, coughing up dust. "Varus?"

"Here." Aphra's voice was strained. She pulled herself out of a pile of twisted aluminum, clutching her ribs. Her silver suit was torn, exposing the dark undersuit beneath. "Broken... maybe just bruised. Suit armor took the brunt."

Varus crawled out from under a collapsed table. He was bleeding from a cut on his forehead, looking dazed but whole. He touched the blood, staring at it on his fingers as if surprised he still bled. In his torn linen shirt, he finally looked the part of a beggar. It was perfect camouflage.

"We're down," Elian said. The wreckage was scattered across a ridge in the middle of the No Man's Land. "We're miles short of the Hind lines."

"Marston?" Aphra asked, looking at the trail of debris leading back up the slope.

Elian shook his head. "He went down with the tail section. You're the last one left, Aphra."

She closed her eyes for a moment, forcing the grief down into the same cold place she kept her fear. When she opened them, they were hard. "Where is Kaelen?"

They found the cockpit embedded in a crater of fused glass. An old Winder anomaly. The canopy was shattered. Kaelen was standing outside, unhurt. He wasn't looking at the wreckage. He was looking into the dark, toward a cluster of iron-bark trees where the mist was gathering.

"Kaelen," Elian called out, limping toward him. "We need to move. The Hinds will send a recovery team to confirm the kill."

Kaelen didn't turn. "I can't go back, Elian."

"You're in shock," Aphra said, stepping forward with a med-stim. "Let me check your vitals."

"It's not shock," Kaelen said softly. He raised his hand. The skin was almost entirely black now, the veins pulsing with a violet light that matched the glow of the Shadows. "The crash... it broke the last tether. I don't belong in the sky anymore."

From the mist, shapes emerged. Tall, flickering silhouettes. The Shadows. They didn't move like enemies; they moved like a retinue waiting for a king.

Varus gasped, stumbling back and crossing himself with a trembling hand. "Demons!"

"No," Kaelen said. "Family."

He turned to face them. The whites of his eyes were gone, flooded by an inky, shifting darkness. He wasn't smiling; he looked at peace.

"The System is re-routing," Kaelen said, his voice sounding like a chorus of static and whispers. "The inventory is flooding the No Man's Land. The balance must be kept. Someone has to direct the flow."

"Kaelen, don't," Elian pleaded. "You're still human. Fight it."

"Go, Cartographer," Kaelen said, stepping backward toward the entities. "Map the world. I will become the world."

The Shadows parted to let him in. Kaelen walked into the mist, and as he did, his form began to flicker, dissolving into the same restless energy as the others. He didn't vanish; he dispersed.

"He's gone," Aphra whispered. She looked devastated. "I brought him here. I did this to him."

"The war did this," Elian said, grabbing her shoulder. "And the war isn't done with us."

A whistle blew in the distance. It was a shrill, mechanical sound. Then, the rumble of engines. Hind tanks were advancing into the Zone.

"We are caught in the middle," Varus said, wiping blood from his eyes. "Between a flooded factory and an invading army."

"And the Horns?" Elian asked, looking back at the distant, burning citadel. "You said they were dead. But hunger is a powerful motivator. What if they find a new reason to fight that isn't you?"

Varus sneered, his arrogance hardening into a shield. "Faith is not a weed, Cartographer. It does not grow wild. It requires a gardener. It requires a voice. I took the voice with me. Behind us, there is only a mob. And mobs do not win wars; they only dig graves."

Elian didn't answer. He looked at the smoke rising in the distance, wondering if the Pontiff had underestimated the resilience of people who had nothing left to lose.

"Then we walk," Elian said, turning toward the sound of the guns. "We have to reach Korm before he triggers the next apocalypse."

They left the wreckage behind, three survivors limping into the dark as the ground beneath them began to vibrate with the waking of new weapons.

Chapter Sixteen

The Wolf of the Rust

THE HORN CITADEL HAD not just fallen; it had ruptured from the inside out.

The collapse of the Apex Spire had sent a shockwave of dust and pulverized stone rolling through the lower districts, coating the city in a shroud of grey snow. But the true devastation wasn't the falling stone; it was the rising steel.

The factory flood had spilled into the Plaza of the Gear, once the market hub for the faithful, bursting from the subterranean freight elevators like arterial spray. It was an avalanche of lethal perfection. Mountains of pristine black rifles, crates of ammunition, and kinetic armor plates were piled against the statues of the saints, burying the stone martyrs in the very tools they had blessed for centuries.

It was a glut. It was a choking hazard.

Thousands of survivors were pressed together in the plaza, coughing in the smog. They were a sea of yellow trench coats and desperate eyes, surging toward the piles, driven by a lifetime of scarcity into a frenzy of acquisition. People were being crushed against the crates, their ribs snapping under the weight of "salvation."

"Do not touch them!" a voice shrieked, cutting through the din.

A Junior Priest, his robes torn and his gas mask cracked, stood atop a teetering stack of ammunition. He was waving a heavy iron censer like a mace, beating back a group of starving workers who were trying to pry open a rations box.

"These are the Tears of the Deep!" the priest screamed, swinging the censer. Embers scattered into the crowd. "They are holy! You are unclean! You cannot touch the inventory until the Pontiff returns to bless it!"

"The Pontiff is gone!" a woman shouted from the crowd, clutching a weeping child to her chest. Her face was grey with ash. "We saw the airship leave! He abandoned us to the fire!"

"Lies!" The priest struck a man in the face with the heavy iron ball. The sound of breaking bone was sickeningly wet. "Back! Pray for forgiveness! The Deep Ones are testing us with abundance!"

The crowd surged back, fearful. Even while starving, the habit of obedience was a heavy chain. They looked at the weapons, tools that could save them, and saw only forbidden idols. They looked at the food and saw poison.

Then, a gunshot cracked through the smog.

It was loud, dry, and decisive. It didn't sound like a prayer; it sounded like a gavel.

The priest stopped mid-sermon. He looked down at his chest, where a red flower was blooming on his white vestments. He looked up, confused, his mouth opening to form a final condemnation, but only blood came out. He toppled off the crate, landing in the mud with a wet slap.

Silence rippled outward from the center of the plaza. The mob parted.

A woman stepped forward. She didn't look like a leader. She looked like the city itself. Hard, scarred, and covered in grease. She wore the heavy rubber apron of a Munitions Overseer, her arms bare and muscular, stained with oil to the elbows. Her hair was shaved close to the scalp, revealing a jagged chemical burn that ran from her temple to her jaw. A souvenir from a burst steam pipe that had taught her more about pressure than any sermon.

In her hand, she held one of the new MK-IV pulse rifles. It was smoking.

"The test is over," she said. Her voice wasn't a scream; it was a grinder. Low, rough, and impossible to ignore.

She climbed onto the crate where the priest had stood. She didn't look at the body; she looked at the crowd.

"My name is Kara," she said. "I ran Shift Four in the Receiving Bay. I know most of you. I signed your ration cards. I docked your pay when you were slow. I am not a priest. I am a mechanic."

She held up the rifle. It gleamed under the flickering streetlights, alien in its perfection.

"For forty years, the priests told us these were magic. They told us they were gifts." She racked the slide of the weapon with a metallic clack. "They lied. I worked the line. I saw the grease. I saw the stamps. This isn't magic. It's a machine. And right now, the machine is vomiting because the people running it ran away."

"The Pontiff..." someone whispered, the name still holding a phantom weight.

"The Pontiff took the Hand!" Kara shouted, pointing a grease-stained finger at the empty sky where the airship had vanished. "He took the only ship capable of flight and left you here to drown in the steel! He traded your lives for his comfort!"

A murmur went through the crowd. It was the sound of a spell breaking.

On the periphery of the plaza, the other priests, dozens of them who had been trying to hold back the tide, looked at each other. They looked at the dead man in the mud. They looked at Kara, who held the rifle not like a relic, but like a tool. And then they looked at the crowd. They did the math.

There was no shout of defiance. One by one, the red robes began to fall. Priests frantically unbuttoned their vestments, letting the heavy, gold-threaded silk drop into the muck. They ripped off their ornate collars. They rubbed soot and grease onto their pale faces, desperate to erase the mark of their caste. In seconds, the Priesthood didn't dissolve; it camouflaged. They became workers again, terrified and anonymous.

"You there!" Kara pointed the rifle at a priest who was halfway out of his robe. "Stop."

The man froze, his hands trembling. He was older, his face soft from decades of good rations.

"You can read the old shipping manifests, can't you?" Kara asked, her voice cutting through the silence. "You know the inventory codes?"

"I... yes," the priest stammered.

"Then keep the robe on," Kara ordered. "I don't need another frightened laborer. I need a clerk. You work for me now. Start cataloging the crates. If the count is off by a single round, I put you in the hopper."

The priest stared at her, then nodded frantically, pulling his robe back up. He wasn't holy anymore; he was useful.

"Look at the sky!" Kara turned back to the crowd, pointing North where the distant Hind flares were painting the clouds red. "They see our smoke. They see our weakness. General Korm is marching right now. He isn't coming to liberate you. He is coming to burn what's left. He is coming to finish the job the famine started."

She kicked the crate beneath her boots. It was stamped WATER - SACRED USE ONLY.

"You have a choice. You can pray to a dead man and starve. Or you can grab a rifle, break open the ration seals, and fight."

She jumped down from the crate, grabbed a pry-bar from her belt, and smashed the lock on the container. Clear, clean water gushed out, the scent of it cutting through the sulfur like a sharp knife.

"Drink!" Kara ordered. "Then arm yourselves. Shift Four is over. The Night Shift starts now."

For a heartbeat, nobody moved. The taboo was too deep. To drink the water, to touch the steel, it felt like suicide. Then, a young man stepped out of the throng. It was Jonas, the soldier from the Receiving Bay. He ran forward, grabbed a rifle, and racked the bolt, mimicking Kara. That broke the dam.

The crowd surged, but not in panic. They swarmed the crates. The hierarchy of the church dissolved, replaced instantly by the brutal efficiency of the factory floor. They organized themselves not into congregations, but into work crews.

"Hold!" A sharp, authoritative bark cut through the commotion.

A squad of Horn Garrison troops pushed through the crowd, led by a Commander in polished armor. He still wore the crest of the Pontiff.

"This is looting!" Commander Harken shouted, his hand on his sidearm. He glared at Kara. "You have no authority here, Overseer. Stand down and surrender the inventory to the Garrison."

Kara didn't flinch. She stepped up to him, invading his space. She smelled of oil and sweat; he smelled of cologne and fear.

"The Garrison?" Kara asked quietly. "Where was the Garrison when the Spire fell? Where were you when the drones started killing the workers in Sector Nine?"

"We were... regrouping," Harken stammered, glancing at the armed mob behind her.

"You were hiding," Kara corrected. She shoved a fresh power cell into his chest plate. "The Pontiff is gone, Harken. The High Command is dead or fled. Look at your men."

Harken looked. His soldiers were eyeing the crates. They were eyeing the water.

"They aren't looking at you, Commander," Kara said. "They're looking at the supply. I control the supply. That means I control the army."

She leaned in close.

"You can be a Commander of the Dead, or you can be a Lieutenant in the Resistance. Pick a side. Now."

Harken looked at the mob. He looked at the rifle in Kara's hand. He realized that the chain of command hadn't just broken; it had been melted down and recast. He took the power cell and slotted it into his rifle.

"What are your orders... Overseer?" Harken asked, his voice stiff.

"Secure the perimeter," Kara said, turning away as if his obedience was a foregone conclusion. "And get these people fed. An empty stomach can't hold a line."

By the time the fires in the lower districts had merged into a wall of flame, the Plaza had transformed into a staging ground. Kara had commandeered the ruined shell of the Railway Station as her command post. Maps were spread over oil drums, held down by heavy-caliber rounds.

"Status on the runners?" Kara demanded.

"Dispatched, Overseer," Jonas reported. He hadn't left her side. He wore a stolen officer's cap pulled low. "We have bikes heading to the Sump Districts. The message is clear: The Pontiff is dead. The Hinds are coming. Fight or die."

"Good," Kara grunted. "But it's not enough. The Hinds have armor. We have rifles and rage, but we don't have weight." She looked at Jonas. "Send a runner to the Crypts."

Jonas froze. "The Crypts? Overseer, that's forbidden ground..."

"There is no Priesthood, Jonas!" Kara slammed her fist onto the oil drum. "There is only the defense. Go to the Crypts. Find the Deep-Walkers."

"The... the Guardians?" Jonas whispered. "But they are sacred. They hold the memory of the First Shifts. They don't fight. They remember."

"They are living vaults of history, Jonas. Three tons of muscle, chitin, and memory. But right now, history doesn't stop bullets. If the Hinds breach the city, the Deep-Walkers will die singing songs to ghosts." She grabbed Jonas by the shoulder, her grip like iron. "Go down there. Wake them up. Tell them the culture is dead. Tell them the history is ending. If they want to preserve the memory of the Horns, they have to survive the night."

"They might kill the messenger," Jonas stammered. "They are... different. They don't think like us."

"They are Horns," Kara said, her voice dropping to a growl. "They are the bedrock. Tell them their children are being slaughtered. Tell them to come up to the light. We need them on the front line." She shoved him toward the door. "Go! And tell them to bring their hammers."

As Jonas sprinted away into the smog, Kara looked out at the burning horizon. She was breaking every taboo, shattering every tradition that had held their society together for seven centuries. She was turning their holy guardians into shock troops. She was burning the library to heat the forge.

She didn't care. Survival had a price, and she was willing to pay it with her soul.

"Adapt or rust," she whispered to the smoke. "Welcome to the new world."

Chapter Seventeen

The Song of Bone

THE DESCENT INTO THE Crypts was not a climb, but a submergence. Jonas didn't just enter the dark; he waded into it, the shadows swirling around him with the viscosity of oil, thick and cold against his skin.

For his entire life, Jonas had lived with a sound in his teeth. It was a low, grinding static that the med-priests called "spiritual corrosion". A term used to dismiss the persistent, agonizing hum that defined his existence. They had bled him, starved him, and once drilled a hole in his helmet to "let the bad air out," seeking a physical culprit for a metaphysical affliction. It hadn't worked. The noise was always there. A phantom frequency that made him clumsy and slow on the line, a constant interference between him and the rest of humanity.

But as he dropped into the waist-deep water of the lower shaft, the static stopped. For the first time in twenty years, the storm inside his skull fell silent.

"Overseer Kara sent me," he whispered. His voice didn't echo. The walls, ancient and thirsty, drank the sound like parched earth drinks rain.

He raised his stolen glow-rod. The blue beam cut through the heavy humidity, revealing a cavern that was not born of steel or hewn stone. The walls were lined with calcified ossuaries, monolithic arches of bone that curved upward to a ceiling lost in a veil of hanging mist. This was no mere bunker; it was the interior of an ancient, gargantuan instrument, silent for eons but still tuned to a fundamental frequency.

Jonas waded forward, his rifle held high, though it felt like a toy in the presence of such antiquity. He didn't need a map. He knew where he was going because the silence was pulling him. Like a compass needle finally finding its true North. In the center of the vaulted chamber, huddled together like sleeping mountains of obsidian, were the sources of the static. They were colossal, mounds of chitinous plating and corded muscle, with six heavy limbs tucked beneath armored carapaces that shimmered with an oily, iridescent sheen.

They weren't sleeping. They were humming.

A low, polyphonic vibration saturated the air. It wasn't a sound Jonas heard with his ears; it was the frequency that had been rattling his bones since birth. It was a chord. Complex, mournful, and terrifyingly beautiful. It sounded like a choir of cellos playing a funeral dirge that had lasted for seven centuries, a sustained note of sorrow echoing from a world that had forgotten its own name.

"I know you," Jonas whispered, tears pricking his eyes. He realized he hadn't been mad; he had simply been a receiver tuned to a broadcast through a mountain of stone.

He stepped closer to the nearest creature. Its carapace was not a smooth shield. It was an illuminated manuscript. Intricate, fractal script. Thousands of lines of microscopic text etched into the living armor, a life's work of memory carved into flesh.

"They aren't weapons." Jonas realized, his fingers trembling as he touched the script. The chitin was warm, pulsing with the same slow, oceanic rhythm as his own heart. "They're books. They are the Archives."

The humming stopped.

A monolithic head shifted with the slow inevitability of tectonic plate movement. Six obsidian eyes, arranged in a hexagonal pattern, blinked open. They didn't glow with the frantic red rage of the war machines upstairs; they glowed with a soft, bioluminescent violet, deep and ancient as the sea.

<Receiver,> a voice echoed in Jonas's head. It was not a voice of words, but a resonance, a harmonic that slid perfectly into the hollow spaces of his mind. <The static clears. You stand in the Echo Chamber. Why do you disturb the Recitation?>

Jonas stumbled back, his splash echoing like a sacrilege. "You... you know me?"

The Deep-Walker shifted, rising to its full height, and water cascaded off its massive flanks like a subterranean waterfall. <We know the noise of your blood. You are the one who listens through the stone. Why are you here, Little Ghost?>

"The Citadel is falling," Jonas stammered, the awe warring with a rising panic. "The Pontiff is dead. The Hinds are coming. The fire is at the gates, and it doesn't care about history."

The creature lowered its head, bringing its massive face inches from Jonas. He could smell the ozone of its thoughts, sharp and clean. <Cycles. The Hinds come. The Horns fall. The wheel turns in the mud. We record the turning. We do not stop it. We are the ink, not the sword.>

"We need you to stop it!" Jonas shouted, his voice cracking against the unyielding quiet. "Overseer Kara sent me. She says the culture is dead. She says if you don't fight, there will be no one left to read the books you've spent your lives writing."

The Deep-Walker recoiled. A ripple of profound distress passed through the other huddling forms, their carapaces clacking together with the sound of dry wood. The hum returned, but it was discordant now, an anxious, frantic thrumming.

<To fight is to forget,> the creature mourned. The voice in Jonas's head was heavy with a sorrow he felt in his own marrow. <To harden the shell for war, we must purge the soft mind. To become the Hammer, we must cease to be the Library. Do you ask us to burn the records to save the shelves?>

Jonas looked at the etched armor, the millennia of history spiraling across the creature's back. He realized the price. The song he had heard his whole life. The song that proved he wasn't crazy, was the soul of his people. If they fought, the song would end forever. He would go back to being just a broken boy in a silent, empty world.

He thought of the starving workers in the plaza. He thought of the priest lying dead in the mud. He thought of Kara standing on the barricade, a single candle against an oncoming storm.

"The building is already burning," Jonas said softly, the words tasting like ash. "If you don't fight, the books burn with it. We don't need you to be a library today. We need you to be a shield."

The Deep-Walker was silent for a long time. A silent debate seemed to pass through the ether, a consensus of ghosts. Jonas felt the weight of their decision pressing on his skull. Not as pain, but as a final, heavy goodbye.

Then, the violet light in its eyes began to shift. It darkened, curdling into a dull, angry red.

On the creature's shell, the intricate script began to smooth out. The chitin shifted and thickened, the delicate, carved words dissolving into jagged ridges of armor plating. The history of the Horns was being erased, formatted in a heartbeat to make room for the rage.

<Then we shall forget.> The voice in Jonas's head became simpler, harder, the poetry evaporating into raw static. <Protect the Hive. Protect the Children. Purge the Memory. Load the Rage.>

The creature let out a roar that shattered the calm of the cavern, a sound that wasn't a song anymore; it was a challenge. It was the sound of a sage choosing to become a beast. Around it, the other Deep-Walkers woke, their eyes snapping to red. They roared in unison, a cacophony of lost potential that shook the bone-arched ceiling.

The lead Walker stepped toward Jonas. It lowered its monolithic body, offering its back.

<Guide us,> it growled, the telepathy now a blunt instrument. <Point us to the enemy. We do not know who they are. We only know how to break them.>

Jonas climbed onto the creature's back, finding a foothold in the jagged ridges where a poem had once been. He felt a sharp, stabbing pain in his temple. The headache was returning, harder than ever. The connection to the Recitation was broken. The song was gone.

But in its place, he felt something else. A cold, distant gaze locking onto him from far below the earth. A watcher.

"Up," Jonas commanded, pointing to the shaft, tears mixing with the soot on his face. "To the surface. We have a war to win."

The Deep-Walkers began to climb, their claws tearing into the stone, leaving deep, ugly scars over the ancient paths they had once walked in peace.

The Deep Core

Miles below, suspended in his column of liquid light, Kaelen flinched.

He felt a sector of the world go dark. The biological archives in the Horn Crypts had just formatted themselves, centuries of lore vanished in a tactical blink. It was a tragedy. A massive loss of data that would have made the old Kaelen weep for the loss of truth.

But Node 7-Alpha didn't weep. He analyzed the void.

And in that new silence, he heard a signal. It was faint, raw, and bleeding with psychic feedback. It wasn't a Molk frequency. It was human, but tuned to the resonance of the stone.

"I see you," Kaelen whispered to the dark, his mind tracing the signal back to the boy riding the beast. "You broke the library, didn't you? You cleared the noise."

He extended his will, brushing against the static in Jonas's mind. It was a raw nerve, exposed and agonizing. Perfect for transmission.

"You want to win the war, Little Ghost?" Kaelen murmured, his voice traveling through the miles of rock not as sound, but as a stabbing migraine. "Then listen to me. I can tell you where to aim."

Kaelen smiled in the dark. He had lost his friends, but the System had just provided him with a perfect instrument.

Chapter Eighteen

The Ghost in the Machine

THE NO MAN'S LAND DID not want them to leave. For two days, they walked. They walked until the soles of their boots were paper-thin and their lungs burned with the persistent metallic rasp of the atmosphere. They navigated the Slag Garden, where twisted iron trees tore at their clothes like the begging hands of the forgotten, and trudged through the Grey Zone, where the silence was so absolute it felt like a weight against their eardrums.

But the silence was a mask. Beneath their feet, the world was chewing.

Elian led the way, his compass in one hand and his charcoal-smudged map in the other. But the parchment was increasingly a relic; the topography was rewriting itself in real-time.

"The terrain isn't just changing; it's being digested," Elian rasped, stopping to lean against a boulder of fused glass. He pointed toward a valley that shouldn't have existed. A jagged, fresh scar in the earth that smoked with residual heat. "The factory is expanding its stomach. That rift wasn't there yesterday because the intake manifolds beneath us just opened. The machine is growing."

As he spoke, the ground ten yards to their left split with a sound like tearing canvas. Steam vented violently, smelling of sulfur and wet iron. The crack widened with a geological groan, swallowing a cluster of petrified trees into the dark.

"Move!" Elian shouted, shoving Aphra away from the crumbling edge. "The crust is thinning!"

They scrambled up a ridge of slate, the ground trembling beneath them as the factory's subterranean expansion consumed another acre of the surface. Aphra stumbled, her breath coming in shallow hitches. Her broken ribs were a constant, grinding agony, but she refused to yield. She looked back at the smoke rising from the distant horizon where the dirigible had met its end.

"We should have found him," she whispered, her hand tightening on her rifle. "Marston. We just left him out there in the dark."

"The section sheared off miles before we hit the ground, Aphra," Elian said gently. "There was nothing left to find. You're the last Recon standing. You have to keep moving, or his sacrifice buys us nothing."

Aphra nodded, swallowing her grief. She turned North, where the sky was choked with an oily black veil. "How far?"

"Ten miles to the Hind outer markers," Elian said. "If the markers still stand."

Varus sat on the ground, massaging his swollen feet. The former High Pontiff looked like a scarecrow fashioned from silk and mud. His fine linen shirt was in tatters, and his face was smeared with the very earth he had once claimed to rule, but his arrogance remained untouched, preserved like a fly in amber.

"They are there," Varus said, his voice dry but certain. "Listen."

Elian strained his ears. Beneath the whistle of the wind, he heard it: a low, rhythmic thumping. Thud. Thud. Thud. It wasn't the harmonic heartbeat of the Molk factory. It was cruder. Heavier. It was the sound of a hammer that didn't know how to stop hitting.

"Artillery," Elian said. "A walking barrage."

"Korm," Aphra added, checking her rifle. It had three charges remaining. "He's clearing the path for the tanks."

"We have to intercept them before they reach the Slag Garden," Elian said, packing his map. "If they cross the Zero Line, the automated defenses... the Shadows... it will be a massacre."

Varus laughed. A dry, brittle sound. "A massacre? For whom, Cartographer? Your General has an army. The Horns have... what?"

"They have survivors," Elian said. "They have desperation."

"They have nothing," Varus corrected, standing up and brushing the dust from his ruined clothes as if preparing for a court audience. "They are sheep without a shepherd. I took the structure with me when I fled. Without my voice, they are just starving animals waiting for the butcher."

"You underestimate them," Aphra said coldly. "We saw the factory output. They are armed with the First Shift."

"Guns are useless without a command to fire," Varus said, his eyes gleaming with the certainty of a man who believed he was indispensable. "Without the Liturgy of the Gear, the battalions will not move. They will wait for a benediction that never comes. They will stand in their trenches and let Korm roll over them because they do not know how to die without permission." He smiled, a cruel, satisfied expression. "Korm will slaughter them. And when he stands over the ashes of my city, he will thank me for the privilege."

Elian looked at the Pontiff, seeing the terminal blindness of a god who had forgotten that his worshippers had teeth. He thought of the young soldier in the receiving bay. The one who had looked at Kaelen. Not with obedience, but with a terrifying hunger.

"You didn't see the eyes of the Shadows, Varus," Aphra said. "And you didn't see the eyes of your own people. Korm isn't fighting sheep. He's fighting the planet."

They reached the edge of the Hind offensive at dusk. It was a terrifying spectacle of industrial power. The Hind army wasn't just a military force; it was a moving city of steel and diesel. Massive Land-Crawlers, tanks the size of cathedrals, belching black smoke that blotted out the stars, crushed the purple vegetation under tracks twenty feet wide. Following them were legions of infantry in heavy plate, their gas masks uniform and skull-like.

The noise was deafening. Engines roared, gears ground, and the artillery hammered the horizon, churning the mud into a soup of fire and earth. It smelled of unburnt fuel and aggressive industry.

"They'll never hear us!" Aphra shouted over the din. "We're ants to them!"

"We have to get to the command track!" Elian yelled back. He pointed to a massive, command-variant Land-Crawler flying the banner of the High Command. "That's Korm's flagship. The Iron Will."

They scrambled down a ridge, waving their arms frantically.

"Cease fire! Friendly! Friendlies on the field!" Elian screamed, waving his cartographer's satchel.

A spotlight from a lead tank swung toward them, blinding in its intensity. "Hold!" a mechanically amplified voice boomed. "Identify!"

"Senior Cartographer Elian Vost!" Elian shouted, shielding his eyes. "Sub-Director Aphra of the Reconnaissance Initiative! And... a high-value prisoner!"

The spotlight didn't waver. A heavy machine gun swiveled, locking onto them with a hydraulic whine. "Vost is listed as MIA," the voice crackled. "Presumed defected. Approach with hands visible. Any sudden movement will result in immediate termination."

They walked forward, hands raised as the mud sucked at their boots. As they reached the line, soldiers in heavy plate surrounded them. They didn't look like men; they looked like rivets that had walked off the hull. Their gas masks were featureless grilles, and their eyes were hidden behind thick, amber lenses that reflected only the flickering fires.

"Take them to the General," a squad leader ordered, shoving Elian forward with the butt of his rifle.

They were marched toward the Iron Will. The air around the massive vehicle was hot and smelled of unburnt fuel. A ramp lowered, and they were shoved into the interior. A bunker on treads. Maps covered the walls. Elian's maps. Now marked with the red ink of current aggression.

General Korm stood at the tactical table. He looked like he had been carved from the same iron as his tank. Half his face was metal, a prosthetic jaw gleaming under the harsh electric lights. He didn't look up as they were thrown to the floor.

"You're alive," Korm grunted, moving a marker on the map. "Disappointing. I had already drafted the eulogy for the 'heroic martyr.'"

"General." Elian stood up, shaking off the soldier who tried to pin him. "You have to stop the advance. The Horn Citadel is destroyed, but the war isn't over. The factory is awake. The No Man's Land is flooded with automated weapons."

Korm finally looked at him. His organic eye was cold; the mechanical one was a glowing red lens. "I know the Citadel is gone, Vost. I saw the smoke. That is why we are marching. The enemy is broken. This is the moment of Continuity. We take the land. We end the threat."

"You aren't walking into a victory!" Aphra shouted, stepping forward despite her pain. "You are walking into a trap! The Horns aren't dead, General; they've just been resupplied. We saw the factory vomit seven centuries of weaponry into their lap. And there are... things out there. Shadows. Drones. Your tanks aren't hunters here. They're prey."

Korm laughed, a sound like grinding gears. He gestured to the racks of fresh, gleaming shells lining the walls of the command deck. Ordnance that hadn't been refilled, but minted new that very morning. Elian looked closer. For twenty years, he had seen Jarek struggling with dented, refilled casings that jammed rifles and killed soldiers. These shells were perfect. The brass was bright, the stamps crisp. There were no weld marks.

"Do you think the mountain only speaks to them?" Korm asked, his voice low and dangerous. "The Southern Line opened yesterday,

Sub-Director. My depots are overflowing. My tanks are full. The Continuity has rewarded our patience with a flood of steel. If the Horns have new teeth, good. It will make the breaking of them more satisfying. Iron does not fail."

He turned to Varus. "And who is this scarecrow? A pet?"

Varus straightened his spine. He might have been in rags, but he remembered how to be a Pontiff. "I am Varus," he said smoothly. "Formerly High Pontiff of the Horn Dominion. And I tell you, General, if you cross that line, you will not find an enemy you can shoot. You will find a hunger you cannot feed."

Korm stared at Varus. For a heartbeat, Elian thought the General might listen. Then, Korm drew his sidearm.

"A Pontiff," Korm sneered. "The head of the snake. Thank you, Vost. You brought me the victory trophy before the battle even started."

He aimed at Varus's head.

"No!" Elian lunged.

BANG.

The shot cracked like a thunderclap in the confined space. It missed Varus by an inch, punching a hole in the tactical map behind him, as Elian slammed into Korm's arm. The recoil threw them both off balance before the guards were on top of them, rifle butts driving Elian and Aphra to the deck.

"Treason," Korm said calmly, holstering his gun. He looked down at Elian, who was gasping for air, blood running from his nose. "Lock them in the brig. Keep the Pontiff alive. I want him to watch his city burn from the front row. Vost and the girl... we'll execute them for desertion once the flag is planted on the Horn ruins."

"You're killing your own men!" Elian screamed as he was dragged away. "Korm! You're marching them into a grinder!"

"The grinder turns, Vost," Korm said, turning back to his map. "It always turns. I'm just the one holding the handle."

The cell door slammed shut, plunging them into darkness. The Iron Will lurched forward, its engine roaring. The Hinds were crossing the Zero Line. The automated war had begun.

Chapter Nineteen

The Dreaming Engine

PAIN WAS A MEMORY, distant and dull, like a thunderclap heard from the bottom of an ocean. Gravity was a suggestion he had chosen to ignore.

Kaelen floated in the center of the Deep Core, suspended in a column of liquid light that tasted of copper and amniotic fluid. He didn't breathe. Breath was a rhythm for things that needed to gasp for survival, for those that feared the cessation of air. Kaelen existed in a state of suspended saturation. The black veins that had once terrified him were now fully integrated, a lattice of living superconductors replacing the fragile, wet copper wiring of his human nervous system.

He was no longer Kaelen the pilot. He was Node 7-Alpha. He was the Bridge.

But the Bridge was full.

Alert: Neural Capacity at ninety-nine percent. Incoming Data Stream exceeds biological buffer.

The warning flashed in his mind, not as text, but as a crushing pressure behind his eyes. The Molk defense protocols were attempting to upload, but his human mind was too cluttered. It was full of useless things. Colors, tastes, the specific way the light hit the clouds over the Western Plateau.

Data possessed a distinct flavor here. The Molk protocols tasted heavy, like iron and gravity, dense, eternal, and cold. His own memories tasted of salt and water, fragile, fleeting, and warm. The System was trying to pour concrete into a glass jar.

Optimization Required. Initiate Archival?

Kaelen hesitated. He knew what the System demanded. It didn't waste data; it viewed his memories as raw artifacts to be cataloged and stored in the deep banks, far from the active processor. To let the mountain in, he had to evict the man.

He looked at a file in his memory: The smell of rain on hot asphalt. Archive.

He felt a cold suction in the center of his mind, and then the sensation was gone. He knew rain existed. He could calculate its pH and velocity. But he could no longer recall the feeling of it on his skin. It was locked away in a server made of obsidian, safe but unreachable.

The sound of his mother's voice singing a lullaby. Archive.

The silence in his head grew louder, waiting to be filled.

The face of the girl he had kissed before deployment. Archive.

Elian's hand gripping his shoulder in the dark tunnel, offering water. The only one who didn't look at him like a broken tool, but like a man. Archive.

He wasn't destroying himself; he was displacing himself. He felt his life being sucked out, file by file, stored in the cold, black quartz of the Core. He carved himself hollow, scoop by scoop, until the pressure behind his eyes faded. Data rushed in to fill the void. Schematics of tectonic plates, firing solutions for magma vents, the history of a dead species. He traded his soul for a manual, locking his humanity in a vault he no longer had the key to.

Around him, the factory screamed with life.

To human eyes, it would have been a hellscape of grinding gears, molten metal, and crushing pistons. But to Kaelen's new eyes, senses that perceived thermal gradients and magnetic flux, it was a symphony. He saw the Shadows, the Harvesters, returning from the surface like antibodies returning to a heart. They flowed through the rock, glowing with the stolen violet energy of the Horn Citadel's grid, carrying the caloric heat of a dying city.

They poured into the Core, discharging their payload.

Thrum. Thrum. Thrum.

The heartbeat of the world quickened. Energy rushed out through the arteries of the factory, waking assembly lines that had been cold since the Second Era. He felt the heat in his own limbs, a fever that wasn't sickness, but power.

But Kaelen looked deeper. He didn't just see the machine; he saw the blueprint. Being part of the System meant inheriting its trauma. The stone remembered everything. It held the echoes of the hands that had carved it. He closed his concept of eyes and let the history of the Molks wash over him.

He saw them. They were not monsters; they were artisans of gravity. Squat, six-limbed creatures with skin like polished granite and eyes that saw tectonic stress lines as clearly as a painter sees color. They didn't build the factory to conquer. They built it to hide.

Kaelen felt their fear. It was a cold, sharp vibration in the rock, a frequency of absolute terror.

The Sky-Breakers. The Silencers. The Winders.

The memory shifted, pulling him back seven hundred years. Kaelen saw the sky tearing open. He saw ships made of impossible, singing glass descending from the stars. They were beautiful, terrible shapes that defied aerodynamics, moving with a silence that hurt the ears.

The Winders weren't invaders; they were curators. They sought to "quiet" the planet. They wanted to iron out the chaotic wrinkles of geology, to pave over the messy, vibrating, biological life of the world with silent, perfect crystal. They didn't want a world; they wanted a marble, a static monument to order.

He saw a Molk parent shielding a child. The "Tone" hit them. There was no blood. There was no fire. In a single, horrifying second, their flesh turned to silicate. They didn't die; they paused forever. They became perfect statues of fear, trapped in a museum they hadn't agreed to join.

The Molks fought back with the only thing they had: Noise. Chaos. Kinetic impact. They built the Engine. They turned the planet into a weapon. They created the "Eternal War" not for conquest, but to produce a shield of debris, radiation, and violence so thick that the Glass Ships couldn't land. They broke their own world to save it.

The War is the Shield, Kaelen realized. The thought rippled through the network, illuminating millions of miles of circuitry. Peace is the danger. If the guns stop, the sky clears. And if the sky clears, the Curators return.

He shifted his focus to the No Man's Land. Through the sensors of the Shadow Swarm, he looked at the Slag Garden. He saw the "anomalies", the fused glass ridges Elian had tried to map. They weren't just wreckage; they were seeds. Buried deep beneath the purple mud, encased in the Winder glass, machines were sleeping. Waiting. They were waiting for the vibration of the surface battles to drop below a certain threshold. Waiting for the silence.

It wasn't just about volume; it was about frequency. The Winders sang a song of perfect order. The Molk Engine was designed to produce an Anti-Harmony. A chaotic, dissonant scream of kinetic energy that disrupted the crystal lattice of the Winder technology.

"They are still here," Kaelen whispered to the darkness, his voice a myriad of overlapping whispers. "The Molks are gone, but the threat remains. The silence is patient."

He looked at the surface again. He saw General Korm's Iron Will churning the mud, marching toward the Horn ruins. He saw Kara's militia digging into the rubble, preparing to fight and die for a city that no longer existed. To Elian and Aphra, this was a tragedy, a senseless slaughter. But from the Core, Kaelen saw it differently.

He saw Korm's tanks not as weapons, but as drumsticks beating the skin of the world. He saw Kara's rage not as defiance, but as percussion. The collision of the two armies wasn't a tragedy; it was a necessary cacophony. The kinetic spike would feed the Shadows. It would scream at the Winder seeds, a lullaby of violence to keep them dormant for another century.

Target Acquired: Hind Command Tank 'Iron Will'. Action: Orbital Strike?

The factory's defense grid offered him a solution. A kinetic rod from a satellite that could vaporize Korm and his entire armored column in a blink. It would be efficient. It would save the Horns. Kaelen's finger hovered over the mental trigger.

No.

If he killed Korm, the Hinds would scatter. The offensive would break. The noise would stop.

"Let them fight," Kaelen commanded, dismissing the targeting solution. His thoughts vibrated through miles of copper wire like a bow across a cello string. "Do not let them win. Victory is silence. The stalemate must hold. The noise must continue."

He checked the logistical flow to the Horn Citadel. The factory was currently in 'Emergency Venting' mode, purging the backlog so fast it was collapsing the very structures he needed to defend. The "miracle" was crushing the believers. Dead soldiers couldn't make noise.

Command Override: Stabilize Output. End Purge Protocol.

He felt the massive pneumatic valves shudder as he forced them to close. He throttled the deluge back into a steady, usable stream. He stopped the flood and started the supply line. He wouldn't just bury them; he would arm them.

Production Order 99-Delta: Regulate flow to Sector Four capacity. Deployment Authorization: Deep-Walker Interface.

Kaelen's mind brushed against the new signals flaring in the Horn Crypts. They were monolithic, ancient biosignatures. The Deep-Walkers. Jonas had woken them. He felt the blankness in their minds where the history used to be. The lobotomy was complete. They were no longer libraries; they were engines of war, waiting for a driver.

I see you, Little Ghost, Kaelen thought, sensing Jonas's raw connection to the beasts. You wiped the drive so I could install the software.

He reached out, not to control them, but to empower them. He opened the subterranean armories beneath the Crypts, releasing kinetic armor plating that would magnetically snap onto the creatures' chitin.

"Arm the beasts," Kaelen commanded the autolanders. "Give them teeth that can chew through Hind steel."

He looked up through the layers of rock toward where his friends were trapped in the belly of the Iron Will.

Simulating Outcome: Scenario 44-Beta. Action: Reveal Truth to Elian. Result: Elian attempts peace. Winder Seeds activate. Extinction Probability: one hundred percent.

Simulating Outcome: Scenario 44-Gamma. Action: Become the Villain. Force Elian to fight the Factory. Result: Elian survives. War continues. Extinction Probability: four percent.

The math was cold, but it was clear.

"Forgive me, Elian," he whispered as the Shadows swirled around him, embracing their master. "You were the only one who looked at me and saw a man, not a circuit. I traded my memory of that kindness to keep the sky burning. And now I have to make you hate me to keep you alive."

Chapter Twenty

The Geometry of Hate

THE INTERROGATION ROOM of the Iron Will was not designed for conversation; it was engineered for confession and the systematic dismantling of the soul.

The walls were unpainted steel, cold and unforgiving, amplifying the mechanical shriek of the Land-Crawler's engines into a deafening resonance that made coherent thought a struggle. Rusty shackles dangled from the ceiling, a hanging promise of pain that served as a psychological weight rather than a physical restraint. The floor was grated, a subtle reminder that anything spilled here, dignity, secrets, or blood, would simply wash away into the oily bilge below. It was a space designed to make a human being feel like a spare part destined for the scrap heap.

Buried deep within the armored gut of the massive vehicle, the room possessed no windows. Only the vibrating bulkheads hummed with the crushing horsepower of the engines. The air was recycled, tasting of diesel fumes, ozone, and the stale sweat of men who knew they were driving into a grave. The initial confidence of the invasion had evaporated, replaced by the grim fatalism of soldiers marching into a fog that smelled of their own obsolescence. A single bulb swung overhead in rhythm with the lurching treads, casting pendulum shadows that made the room feel as if it were breathing.

General Korm sat on one side of the bolted-down table. His mechanical eye whirred softly, the lens expanding and contracting as it focused on the prisoner. Its red light was the only splash of color in a world of grey metal.

High Pontiff Varus sat opposite him. His hands were bound with industrial zip-ties that bit into his wrists. His robes, once the gilded envy of a city, were now merely dirty rags clinging to a starving frame. He looked less like a religious leader and more like a scarecrow that had collapsed into the mud.

"You look small," Korm said. It wasn't an insult; it was a tactical observation, delivered with the flat affect of a commander assessing a target. "For forty years, I have imagined the High Pontiff as a giant. A monster breathing smoke and eating steel. But you are just a man who needs a bath."

"And you look heavy," Varus replied, his voice raspy but steady. He leaned forward, the chains clinking against the table's edge. "Half iron. Half meat. Do you even remember which part is the human part, General? Or did you amputate that too in the name of Continuity?"

Korm slammed his fist onto the table. The sound rang like a bell in the confined space, a sudden violence that made the shadows jump.

"Do not speak to me of Continuity. I am the fist that protects the Hind. I have captured the enemy's king. The game should be over." Korm leaned closer, the heat of his cybernetics radiating across the metal. "So tell me, Pontiff... if the King is in chains, why is the Kingdom still fighting?"

"King?" Varus spat the word like it was a piece of gristle. He sat up, the zip-ties straining as he squared his shoulders, regaining a flicker of the presence that had held a starving city in thrall. "Do not insult me with such a small, terrestrial title, General. A king rules borders. A king rules tax codes and conscription lists. A king can be beheaded and replaced by any fool with a bloodline." He leaned in, meeting the red glow of Korm's eye without blinking. "I am the High Pontiff. I do not rule a kingdom; I rule a necessity. I am the Voice that turns starvation into piety. I am the architect of their reality. When a king dies, the kingdom mourns. If I fall, the sky itself should collapse. So do not ask me about kings."

Korm stared at him, taken aback by the venom. "And yet," Korm said, sliding a reconnaissance photo across the table, "the sky has not collapsed. And your people are still fighting."

Varus looked at the photo, his anger faltering into confusion. "Fighting? My city is destroyed. My people are scattered. They are eating rats in the gutters."

"Your people are holding the Northern Ridge," Korm corrected. "They have dug in. They are armed with weapons my scanners have never seen before. Rifles that punch through Class-A plate like it's wet paper. And they are led by... something else." He tapped a blur on the photo. "Beasts. Massive, chitin-armored nightmares that tear my light tanks apart. They don't move like machines; they move like predators."

Varus looked at the grainy image. He saw the blur of a Deep-Walker smashing through a Hind barricade. He saw the flash of the new pulse rifles. His face went pale, not with fear, but with a terrible realization.

"The Deep-Walkers," Varus whispered, his voice a mix of horror and awe. "Someone woke the Guardians. Someone broke the seals on the Crypts."

"Who?" Korm demanded. "Who is issuing the orders? I have you. Who is left?"

"I am cycling through the candidates now," Varus said, his voice gaining strength as he engaged his analytical mind. "General Vult is a drunkard who commands from a bunker five miles deep; he wouldn't dare open a Crypt. Commander Harken? A parade soldier who cares more about the polish on his boots than the line. He lacks the imagination for heresy. The High Bishops? They are theologians, General, not tacticians. They faint at the sight of unrefined oil." He looked up, meeting Korm's gaze with genuine bewilderment. "There is no one in the chain of command with the spine for this. The Priesthood is ceremonial. The bureaucrats are cowards. There is no one else capable of this sacrilege."

"There is always someone else!" Korm roared, standing up. The room shrank around them. "An army does not fight without a head! Chaos does not hold a ridge!"

"Unless the body has learned to hate on its own," Varus said softly. He looked up at Korm, and a dark recognition passed between them. For centuries, they had been the twin poles of the world: the General and the Pontiff. The Iron and the Smoke. They fed each other. Korm needed the Horns to justify his budget, his armor, and his absolute authority. Varus needed the Hinds to justify his prayers, his shortages, and his control.

"We are the same," Varus whispered, a bitter smile touching his lips. "We are two old men shouting at a storm, pretending we control the wind. But the wind is blowing without us now, General. We are obsolete."

Korm sat back, the silence stretching thin, punctuated only by the thrum of the treads eating the mud. He looked at the photo, then at Varus. He hated the Pontiff, but he hated the unknown more. The unknown was a variable he couldn't shoot.

"Guard," Korm barked at the door. "Bring the Cartographer. And the woman."

Elian and Aphra were shoved into the room a moment later. They looked exhausted and bruised, their clothes stiff with the grime of the journey. But their eyes were sharp; they saw the tension in the room immediately. They saw the stalemate of two leaders who had lost control of their narratives.

"He doesn't believe you," Elian said, looking at Korm.

"He doesn't understand," Korm corrected, his mechanical eye whirring. "He claims he doesn't know who is leading his army. He claims he doesn't know where the new weapons come from. He claims he is innocent of his own war."

"He's telling the truth," Elian said. He walked to the table, ignoring the guards who tensed. "He doesn't know because he was never in charge. And neither are you."

Elian reached into his satchel. He didn't pull out a weapon; he pulled out a sheaf of papers, charcoal sketches, maps, and notes scribbled in the dark of a Molk tunnel. The paper was dirty and torn, yet more valuable than the tank they stood within.

"General, you fight on maps drawn in the year 520," Elian said, spreading a large, smudged sheet across the table, covering Korm's reconnaissance photos. "This is the map of 700."

Korm looked at the paper. His face darkened. His hand went to his sidearm. "That is an unauthorized survey," Korm growled, his voice dropping to a dangerous mechanical rumble. "To draw a new line is to deny the Doctrine of Continuity. To present this to me is treason, Vost. I could shoot you where you stand."

"I know," Elian said, not flinching, though Aphra tensed beside him. "The Doctrine says the world is static. The Doctrine says we hold the Vrail River. But look at the map, General. Look at the treason. Look at the world as it is, not as you were told to see it." Elian stabbed his finger onto the paper. "This is the No Man's Land." Elian pointed to the top layer. "Where we are now. Where you are driving your tanks." He traced a line downward, cutting through the strata of the earth. "This is the Deep Road. A transit tunnel twenty miles down. We walked it. It connects your territory to his. It's a highway, General. While your men died for inches of mud, the real enemy was moving miles beneath your boots." He traced deeper, into a massive, swirling knot of charcoal darkness. "And this... this is the Factory. The Iron Harvest."

Korm's finger hovered over the trigger of his pistol. He was trembling, a glitch in his internal logic. The fanatic in him wanted to purge the heresy; the soldier in him stared at the lines, recognizing the tactical reality his doctrine had forced him to ignore.

"The weapons," Korm said quietly, releasing his grip on the gun. "The fresh rifles the Horns are using."

"Made here." Elian tapped the factory. "By the millions. Automated. The Horns don't build them. They just catch them when they fall out of the chute."

"And the Hinds?" Korm asked, his voice dangerous.

"Where do you think the heavy plate for your tanks comes from, General?" Elian asked. "The Southern Mines? Have you ever been there? Or do the shipments just arrive on the automated rail lines, right on schedule, untouched by human hands?"

Korm went still. He thought of the endless supply trains. The unceasing logistics. The seamless continuity of the war that had always seemed too perfect for a dying empire.

"We are being farmed," Aphra said, stepping up beside Elian. "Both sides. You aren't enemies. You're just the left hand and the right hand of the same machine. You are components in a closed loop."

"Why?" Varus whispered, staring at the map. "Why build such a thing?"

"To make noise," Elian said. He looked at Korm. "The war isn't about victory, General. It's about volume. The kinetic energy. The explosions. The screams. It keeps the ground shaking."

"Why does the ground need to shake?" Korm asked.

"To keep the Silencers away," Elian said, pointing to the blank spots in the No Man's Land. "The archives speak of the Winders, but they also call them 'The Silencers.' We always thought it was a name. But what if it's a description? They hate the noise. As long as we fight, they stay dormant. If we stop... the silence brings them back."

The room was silent, punctuated only by the thud of distant artillery. Korm looked at the map. He saw the vast, intricate trap they had all been born into. He saw the futility of every medal on his chest, each ribbon representing a thousand dead men who had died not for a cause, but for a quota.

"They spent us," Korm whispered. "They spent my divisions like currency to pay a debt I didn't know I owed."

Varus watched him. He recognized the shift in the General's posture, the moment a believer becomes an apostate.

"They used my loyalty as fuel," Korm growled. "And they used your faith as a lubricant, Pontiff."

"It would seem," Varus said, his voice quiet and deadly, "that we have both been poor stewards of our own power." He leaned forward. "If the machine wants noise, General... perhaps we should give it a scream it will not forget."

Korm looked at Varus. For the first time, he saw the only other man in the world who understood the scale of the betrayal. "So," Korm said. "If I win, the world ends. If I lose, my people die. It is a poisonous choice."

"There is a third option," Elian said. "We stop fighting the distraction and we start fighting the source. We break the machine that's playing us. We attack the Factory Vents."

"The Vents," Varus murmured. "The Lungs of the Deep Ones. The priests said the earth breathed fire there."

"They weren't sacred," Elian said. "They were exhaust ports. And if we plug them, the machine chokes."

Korm stood up. The red light of his eye stabilized, locking onto a new target. He wasn't a philosopher; he was a soldier who had just been given an enemy.

"Get this trash off my table." Korm swept the old tactical maps, the holy documents of his Doctrine, onto the floor. They fluttered down like dead leaves. He looked at Elian. "Show me where the vents are, Cartographer. If the machine wants a war... let's give it one."

Chapter Twenty One

The Wolf at the Door

THE NORTHERN RIDGE WAS no longer a mere geographical fact of stone and soot; it had transformed into a heaving lung of cinders that didn't simply burn, it shrieked with the raw, metallic agony of a world being flayed alive.

The air was a solid wall of dissonance, the shriek of tearing metal, the rhythmic bass-thrum of artillery, and the wet, biological roar of entities that had no business walking in the daylight.

Kara stood atop the shattered remains of a gargoyle, peering through the acrid, oily smoke. Below her, the Horn defense line was a chaotic scar across the ruins, cobbled together from crushed vehicles, stone saints, and crates of factory-fresh weaponry that still carried the cold scent of the deep earth. The line held, but the friction was stripping the gears of their sanity.

"Range Mark Four!" she screamed, her voice cracking against the roar. "Focus fire on the crawler tracks! Immobilize the weight!"

A hundred meters down the slope, a Hind light tank churned the debris, its engines whining as it attempted to scale the rubble. It never reached the crest. A squad of Kara's militia, armed with the new MK-IV pulse rifles, unleashed a torrent of blue energy. The concentrated fire didn't just dent the plate; it fused the drive-trains into slag. The tank spun helplessly on a broken tread, exposing its vulnerable flank.

"Now!" Kara signaled, her arm cutting through the smog. "Release the hammer!"

The shadows beneath the collapsed cathedral archway didn't just shift; they fractured. A monolithic shape emerged, tearing through the masonry as if the stone were parchment. It moved on six powerful legs, its body encased in chitinous plates that gleamed like wet obsidian armor that appeared denser and more resilient than any Hind steel.

A Deep-Walker.

The creature didn't merely roar; it emitted a frequency, a low, vibrating resonance that rattled the marrow in every soldier's bones. It charged with a terrifying, insectoid grace, slamming into the immobilized tank and flipping the thirty-ton machine onto its roof.

Kara watched the beast for a second too long. She saw its eyes. A dull, hungry red, where the ancient stories promised a soft violet. There was no poetry in its movements, no memory in its gaze. She had traded the history of her people for a heavy weapon, and the hollow ache in her chest told her she might never be forgiven for the bargain.

The militia erupted in a ragged, desperate cheer, but Kara didn't join them.

"Don't celebrate!" she barked, leaping down from her perch. She grabbed a soldier who had raised his rifle in premature triumph and shoved him back into the safety of the trench. "Reload! They have legions in reserve! We have nothing but the time we steal!"

"Overseer!" Jonas ran up, lugging a heavy container. He dropped it at her feet, his chest heaving, his face a mask of sweat and soot. "Fresh delivery from the Plaza lift. It arrived seconds ago."

Kara looked at the box. Unlike the dented, scorched wreckage of the initial "Rapture" flood, this container was pristine. A fresh laser-etching on the lid read: SECTOR 4 - KINETIC/ ARMOR-PIERCING. URGENT.

"The elevators." Jonas panted, wiping grime from his eyes. He paused, his expression shifting from exhaustion to a strange, haunted clarity. "They changed, Kara. An hour ago, they were shaking the mountain apart. But now... I can hear the hum again. The static in my head... it's not noise anymore. It's a pulse. It's him."

"Him?" Kara asked, her hand pausing on the crate's latch.

"The Pilot," Jonas whispered. "Kaelen. I don't know how I know, but the rhythm of the lifts... it matches the rhythm he used to have. Someone is driving the train, Kara, and I think he's remembering us."

Kara stared at the smooth operation of the lift mechanisms. It felt different than the chaotic religious ecstasy of the previous days. It felt intelligent. It felt as if a cold, calculating eye was watching the battle from below, adjusting the variables of their survival.

"The machine isn't just awake." Kara realized, a chill chasing the heat of the battle from her skin. "It's lucid. And it's taking sides."

"They saw the tanks," Jonas said, grabbing the heavy ordnance. "They knew exactly what we needed."

"Then we use it," Kara said, though the precision of the delivery frightened her. A chaotic god was manageable; a competent one was an existential threat. She loaded a shell into a heavy launcher. "Target the lead Crawler! Break the formation!"

Then, the shelling stopped.

It didn't taper off; it ceased with a suddenness that made the silence feel like a physical blow. The constant thud of the Hind artillery fell into a hollow void. The world seemed to hold its breath.

"They're reloading," a militia captain suggested nervously.

"No," Kara said, climbing back onto the gargoyle. She raised her binoculars. "This was a command."

In the valley below, the massive Hind army was shifting. The Land-Crawlers were reversing, their engines growling like cornered beasts. But they weren't facing the Horn ruins anymore. They were turning their backs to the Citadel.

"They're pivoting," Kara whispered.

She watched as the Iron Will, General Korm's massive command tank, swung its primary turret away from the Horn lines. It pointed

North, toward the empty, scarred expanse of the No Man's Land. Toward the Slag Garden.

"What are they doing?" Jonas asked, his antennae twitching as he felt the shift in the earth's vibration. "There's nothing out there but salt and ghosts."

"I don't know," Kara said. The hair on her arms stood up. It wasn't relief she felt; it was a deep, primal unease. The enemy had found a target they hated more than her.

The Hind army unleashed a volley. Five hundred guns fired in a single roar. The shells screamed over the Horn lines, arching high into the Grey Zone to impact miles away. The ground groaned beneath the impact.

"They're shelling the empty mud," Jonas said, his confusion turning to an odd sense of insult.

Kara watched the distant explosions. She saw flashes of blue light erupting from the ground where the ordnance hit. Not the orange of fire, but something venting from beneath the crust.

"They aren't shelling the mud." Kara realized. "They're shelling the vents. They're attacking the source of the supply."

She lowered the binoculars. The Hinds had stopped trying to kill her people. They had turned their backs on a seven-hundred-year-old enemy to shoot at the ground.

"Overseer?" Jonas asked. "Do we pursue? We could break them here."

Kara looked at her ragged army, armed with weapons delivered by a ghost. She looked at the Deep-Walkers, who were now pawing at the ground, their red eyes fixed on the distant tremors.

"No," Kara said. "We hold the line. We let them shoot at the ghosts."

She watched the factory drones buzzing away into the distance, joining the defense of the No Man's Land. The logic of the battlefield had shifted. The Hinds weren't fighting the Horns; the Horns weren't fighting the Hinds. They were all just fleas on a dog that had finally started to scratch.

"Something has changed, Jonas," Kara said, gripping her rifle until the metal bit into her palm. "The war isn't about us anymore. We've been demoted to spectators."

She looked at the burning horizon, realizing that for the first time in history, the Horns were not the most dangerous thing on the battlefield.

"Dig in," she ordered, her voice flat. "And watch. I think the world is about to break open."

Chapter Twenty Two

The Weaver of Scars

PAIN WAS NOT A SENSATION; it was a topographic map, a cartography of suffering etched into the very mantle of the world.

Deep in the obsidian womb of the Core, Kaelen did not scream when the Hind shells struck the surface vents miles above. Instead, he watched a sector of his peripheral vision bloom into a flashing, critical red. He experienced the impact as a bruised rib, a phantom fracture in a body that had long since surrendered its flesh. The shockwaves traveled through the bedrock, vibrating against his new, copper-laced nervous system like a bow drawn across a raw, exposed nerve. Every impact was a data point, a jagged spike of seismic energy he was forced to absorb and redistribute before the pressure cracked his liquid sanctuary.

He floated in the suspension field, saturated in a bath of liquid data that tasted of ozone and ancient amniotic fluid, but he was no longer alone.

The Shadows swirled around him, a vortex of hungry, violet smoke. They were no longer merely feeding on the reactor; they were feeding on him. On his commands, on his burgeoning rage. They were his nerves, stretching out through miles of copper wire and stone. They whispered in a thousand dead dialects. The voices of those distilled into the System over seven centuries. They whispered a chorus of appetites demanding direction. They tasted of cold ash and static, an eternal winter of the soul.

<We burn, Weaver,> the Shadows hissed in his mind, their voices overlapping like the dry vibration of insect wings. <The iron bugs

above... they crush the lungs. They choke the breath of the Deep. Give us the fire.>

"Stop it," Kaelen whispered. His voice was no longer a single human chord; it was a multitude, a harmonic resonance that shook the suspension fluid. "You are breaking the seal. You are inviting the silence."

He extended his awareness upward, riding the fiber-optic nerves of the network. He saw through the eyes of the surviving drones, witnessing flickering glimpses of a world on fire. He saw the Iron Will, a lumbering iron beetle, and the line of Hind tanks hammering the Slag Garden. They were trying to suffocate the factory, burying the thermal exhaust ports under tons of displacement, oblivious to the fact that they were capping a volcano of their own making.

He shifted his focus North, to the Horn ruins.

He felt the biosignatures of the Deep-Walkers. They were burning bright and hot, fueled by the sacrifice of their own memories, their chitinous hearts beating in a frantic, war-coded rhythm. And riding the lead beast was a spark, faint, raw, and bleeding with psychic static.

The Little Ghost.

Kaelen focused on Jonas. He didn't just watch the boy; he invaded him. He slid his consciousness into the headache that had plagued Jonas his entire life, fitting himself into the neural gaps like a key into a lock.

<Eyes up, Little Ghost,> Kaelen transmitted, his presence a cold pressure behind Jonas's eyes.

On the surface, Jonas gasped, clutching his head as blood began to leak from a nostril, but he did not fall. He looked where Kaelen directed him. Kaelen felt the boy's fear. It tasted of salt, adrenaline, and a desperate, child-like hope. And the boy, in turn, felt Kaelen's vast, cold geometry. It was a violation of the individual, a merging of the biological and the geological that left Jonas's mind reeling.

<Mark the line,> Kaelen commanded, pulling the data from Jonas's optic nerves. <Show me where your people end and the enemy begins. Show me the targets for the earth to eat.>

Through Jonas's eyes, Kaelen saw the battlefield with chilling clarity. He painted the Horn lines in safety-green and the Hind lines in terminal-red.

The Horns are safe. Kaelen calculated, his humanity flickering like a dying bulb before the cold logic of the system took over. The boy and the beasts are holding the door. That leaves the Hinds.

Korm thought he was starving a beast. He didn't realize he was suffocating the planet's immune system. And the system possessed antibodies that hadn't been deployed in seven hundred years. Kaelen looked deeper into the factory, into the sealed vaults that even the Shadows avoided. He required more than energy; he needed mass. He needed hands that could move the foundations of the world.

"Wake them," Kaelen commanded the Shadows. "Wake the Stone Sentinels."

In the deep maintenance bays, the walls themselves began to groan. The Stone Sentinels were not separate entities; they were the architectural columns of the factory itself. Monolithic, six-limbed constructs carved from living granite, holding up the roof of the world. To move them was to risk the ceiling coming down. It wasn't a summoning; it was a controlled demolition.

"Move," Kaelen ordered, throwing the safety protocols aside. "Even if the roof falls."

Violet energy surged into the stone. Dust that had settled for a millennium cracked and fell away in sheets. Stone ground against stone with a sound like tectonic plates shifting. A scream of friction that shook the cavern and resonated in Kaelen's own teeth. He felt the weight of their limbs, the grinding resistance of their joints, as if his own body were made of granite. The Stone Sentinels opened eyes that glowed with the same flat, grey light as the Core.

<We serve,> the Sentinels resonated, their thoughts slow, heavy, and enduring as mountains. <The burden shifts.>

"The vents are rusted shut," Kaelen told them, the effort of directing them making his human heart flutter in its suspension. "Force them. Bleed the pressure into the intruders."

The warning flashed in Kaelen's mind, cold and blue: Seismic vibration approaching Critical Threshold.

He shifted his focus to the "Blind Spots", the Winder Seeds. The bombardment was shaking them, the glass shells vibrating at a frequency that heralded the return of the Silencers. Kaelen dove into the Archive, accessing the file he had hidden earlier: The History of Silence.

The memory hit him like a physical blow.

Year Zero. The Sky Tears Open.

He wasn't Kaelen anymore. He was a Molk Elder. The sky above wasn't grey with smog; it was blue, a terrifying, empty clarity. And descending from that clarity were the Ships. They didn't fire lasers; they didn't drop bombs. They emitted a Tone. It was a sound so pure, so mathematically perfect, that it arrested atomic motion.

Kaelen watched as the Molk cities didn't burn, they crystallized. Living rock turned to brittle glass. Flesh turned to silicate statuary. Entropy died, replaced by a horrifying, static perfection. The Winders were bringing "Peace." They were bringing the stillness of a frozen lake.

Kaelen snapped back to the present. The liquid light around him roiled.

"Peace is death," he hissed, his voice echoing through the millions of miles of the network. "Silence is glass."

He looked at the tactical map of the surface. Elian was up there. Elian, who wanted to map the truth. Elian, who thought stopping the war was an act of mercy.

"You are a fool, Cartographer," Kaelen murmured, a tear of black fluid leaking from his eye and dissolving into the suspension fluid. "You want to clear the sky. You don't know what looks back from the blue."

Kaelen made his decision. He could not stop Korm with brute force; the factory was designed to supply armies, not fight them directly. But he could redirect the waste. He could bleed the pressure. He accessed the tectonic stabilizers.

Command Override: Node 7-Alpha. Action: Venting Protocol - Emergency Purge. "Sentinels," Kaelen commanded, the word causing a convulsion in his chest. "Open the Geothermal Siphon. Flood the Grey Zone."

Miles below the surface, the stone constructs braced their limbs against the rusted manual override wheels of the magma valves. They pushed. The metal groaned, then shrieked. Decades of oxidation snapped like gunfire. The valves turned.

The factory roared a sound of liberation. Deep beneath the crust, the pressure released. Kaelen felt the heat rising in his own veins, a burning fever that started in his marrow and threatened to boil the amniotic fluid.

It wasn't just magma. It was slag. It was a liquefied graveyard. It was the melted remains of every sword, shield, shell casing, and bone that had ever been fed into the earth by the Scavengers. It was a slurry of unmade history, toxic, radioactive, and heavy with the weight of a thousand failed battles. He was about to turn the No Man's Land into a volcanic pressure cooker. It would wipe out half the Hind army. It might even kill Elian.

But it would keep the Seeds warm. It would keep the noise going.

"I am the Weaver," Kaelen said, the Shadows swirling around him in a protective vortex of violet light. "I will scar this world so deeply that the silence can never take root. I will be the monster that keeps the stars away."

He closed his eyes and initiated the purge.

The ground above began to tremble. Not from artillery this time, but from the waking, industrial rage of the earth itself.

Chapter Twenty Three

The Bleeding Earth

THE HEAVENS HAD BEEN traded for a ceiling of screaming iron. The bombardment was a masterpiece of industrial desecration, a symphony played on five hundred Hind artillery pieces that fired in a synchronized roar. From the command deck of the Iron Will, Elian watched as the sky became a jagged shroud of charcoal smoke, torn apart every few seconds by the incandescent trails of shells arching toward the heart of the No Man's Land. The concussion didn't merely rattle the teeth; it juddered through the marrow, resetting the very rhythm of the heart to the cadence of the guns. The air inside the tank was a stagnant cocktail of recycled breath, burning insulation, and the sharp, copper tang of adrenaline.

Impact.

Miles away, the Slag Garden vanished beneath a heavy blanket of fire. The monolithic cooling towers of the Molk Factory, which had once stood as rusted mountains of defiance, began to crumble. Concrete pulverized into a grey mist. Steel twisted with the effortless frailty of wet rope. The vents that had been vomiting weapons and drones were being choked by their own shattered debris.

"Direct hit on Sector Four," a comms officer shouted, his voice cracking with the strain of the noise. "Thermal output dropping. The vents are sealed!"

General Korm stood at the viewport, his hands clasped behind his back. The red lens of his mechanical eye whirred, recording the annihilation with a cold, geometric satisfaction. He was a conductor watching his orchestra reach its final, crushing crescendo.

"The machine breaks," Korm stated, his voice a low rumble beneath the thunder. "Iron beats stone. Continuity is restored."

Elian looked at the seismic monitor on the primary console. The needle wasn't dropping. It was vibrating so violently that it blurred, scratching a jagged, black hole through the paper drum.

"It's not breaking," Elian warned, backing away from the console as if the data itself were radioactive. "You're capping a pressure cooker, General. If you seal those vents, the heat has to find a new path. The physics of this place do not care about your victory."

"Let it burn underground." Korm dismissed him, not turning from the window. "Let the Molks choke on their own smoke."

"General!" the sensor officer yelled, clutching his headset as static screamed through the line. "Ground temperature is rising! Rapidly! Sector One through Ten... everywhere. The sensors are melting!"

Elian looked out the window. The purple mud of the No Man's Land was beginning to bubble. It started as small pockets of gas, hissing like kettles. Then, the puddles began to boil. The twisted iron trees of the Slag Garden didn't burn; they began to glow a dull, furnace-red from the roots up.

"It's a purge," Aphra whispered, her face illuminated by the rising, sickly glow from the earth. She checked her wrist readout, her eyes widening. "Kaelen isn't just venting excess heat. He's weaponizing the coolant lines. He's dumping the core."

The earth didn't crack; it liquefied.

A mile in front of the Hind vanguard, a geyser of superheated steam erupted. It wasn't a puff of smoke; it was a column of white violence a mile high. The sound hit the Iron Will a second later, a shriek that rattled the bolts in the hull and brought Varus to his knees.

Then, the magma came.

It wasn't the slow, red lava of a natural volcano. It was Slag, the liquefied graveyard of unmade history. It was a black, industrial slurry of molten rock, radioactive waste, and the melted remains of every sword, shield, and bone that had been fed into the hoppers for seven centuries. It smelled of burning battery acid, copper, and ancient sorrow. It burst from the ground in a tidal wave, moving faster than a tank could drive and hotter than any furnace.

"Reverse engines!" Korm roared, grabbing the comms handset. "Seventh Heavy, fall back! Pattern Delta!"

"General, the tracks are melting!" The voice on the radio was Commander Hrix, leader of the vanguard. "It's not just heat! It's corrosive! It's eating the hulls!"

"Fall back, Hrix!" Korm screamed, losing his composure for the first time. "Abandon the line!"

"We can't move!" Hrix's voice distorted into a shriek of static. "It's inside! It's inside the..."

The transmission cut.

Elian watched in horror as the pride of the Hind army was consumed. The massive Land-Crawlers were useless against the waking rage of the earth. The black sludge washed over them like a rising tide, dissolving armor into the flow. The tanks simply sank, boiling away into the slurry of their own ancestors.

"They're melting," Varus whispered, clutching his holy symbol with trembling fingers. "The earth is eating them. The Deep Ones have rejected us."

"It's not the earth," Elian said, thinking of Kaelen in the dark, his mind fused with the Stone Sentinels. "It's a defense mechanism. We threatened the Shield. Now the Shield is removing the threat."

The Iron Will groaned as its massive treads fought for traction in the dissolving soil. Inside the command deck, the temperature was rising to lethal levels. Alarms screamed: Hull Temperature Critical. Air Filtration Failing.

"We can't outrun it," Aphra said, looking at the tactical map. "The flow is spreading too wide. It's going to wash the entire Grey Zone clean. Even if the heat doesn't kill us, the toxic plume will."

"Turn us," Elian ordered, shoving the navigator aside. "Don't run from it. Turn East. Toward the high ground. The Ridge of Silence."

"That's into the impact zone!" Korm shouted, drawing his sidearm. "You are steering us into the fire!"

"The Ridge is fused glass!" Elian yelled back, meeting the General's mechanical eye. "It's Winder material! It has a higher melting point than the bedrock! It's the only thing that won't dissolve!"

Korm hesitated, looking at the wall of black fire approaching. He looked at the pistol in his hand, then at the melting horizon.

"Do it," Korm rasped.

The massive tank slewed sideways, its engines screaming as it fought the current of the sludge. It climbed the slope of the Grey Zone, narrowly missing a fountain of slag that incinerated a squad of infantry.

They slammed onto the ridge, a long, jagged spine of translucent material. The impact was frictionless; the tank slid onto the surface, drifting like a puck on ice.

The sludge hit the ridge a second later and parted. It didn't melt the glass; it slid off it. The Winder material ignored the heat, remaining cool and slick, defying the thermodynamics of the disaster. The Iron Will shuddered and stopped, marooned on an island of cold starlight in a sea of fire.

Silence fell over the bridge. The only sound was the hissing of cooling metal.

"My army," Korm whispered. He touched the window, leaving a greasy smear on the glass. "Seven hundred years of tradition. Gone in minutes."

"Not gone," Aphra said softly. "Recycled."

Elian walked to the window. The Purge had done exactly what Kaelen intended. It had wiped the board. The factory vents were cleared, melted open by the flow. The noise of the artillery had stopped, replaced by the low, resonant hum of the cooling slag. But the Purge had stripped the topsoil of the No Man's Land, washing away centuries of mud and ruins.

Elian stared at the ground below the ridge. The earth was gone. And something else was shining in the twilight.

It was vast. Smooth. Perfect.

It reflected the fires of the dying tanks without a scratch, absorbing the chaos and returning only a cold, perfect white light. It lay beneath the Slag Garden like a buried moon.

"General," Elian said, his voice trembling. "Look down."

Embedded in the earth, revealed by the fire, was a structure of singing glass. It wasn't a ruin. It was a Seed. And it was pulsating with a soft, pale light that seemed to stop the smoke in the air.

"The silence didn't wake it up." Elian realized. "We knocked on the door too hard."

Chapter Twenty Four

The Singing Glass

THE WORLD HAD ENDED, and it was beautiful. Elian stood on the hull of the Iron Will, the residual heat of the cooling slag radiating through the soles of his boots. The sky above was a bruise of purple and black smoke, but the ground beneath him was made of starlight.

The Geothermal Purge had receded, leaving the valley stripped to the bedrock. In the place of the mud and the corpses lay the Seed. It was immense. A dome of translucent, singing silicate that spanned three miles. It pulsed with a soft, rhythmically shifting light, pale blue, then white, then a terrifyingly absolute transparency. It didn't reflect the fire; it absorbed it, swallowing the chaos and returning nothing but a cold, flat perfection.

"It's not a building," Aphra whispered, standing beside him. She had removed her helmet; the air was toxic, yet she seemed indifferent to the risk. She stared at the readings on her wrist comp, which were flatlining. "The sensors aren't broken, Elian. They just... stopped. There is no variance. No vibration. It's a lung. Look. It's breathing."

The surface of the glass shifted by millimeters with every pulse. And with every breath, it emitted a sound. It wasn't a noise; it was a frequency of absolute order. It didn't merely ring in Elian's ears; it vibrated in the marrow of his bones, attempting to align the chaotic carbon atoms of his body into a perfect, static grid. It slowed his pulse and made the act of inhaling feel messy and redundant. It was a lullaby that promised the end of struggle, the end of self. It was the sound of entropy dying.

"The Silencers," Elian said, the old archival term tasting like ash in his mouth. "Kaelen was right. They aren't dead. They're just waiting for us to stop screaming."

General Korm climbed out of the hatch. He looked like a ghost haunting his own armor. His mechanical eye was cracked, the servos whirring in a stuttering rhythm as they tried to sync with the Tone. He looked down at the grave of his army. He listened for the war. The noise that had defined his existence since birth, but found only the Tone.

"Where are they?" Korm croaked, stripped of all command authority. "Where are my men?"

"They are part of the crust now, General," Varus said softly. The former Pontiff sat on the turret, turning a piece of slag over in his hand like a rosary bead. "Dust to dust. Iron to rust. It is a cleaner god than the one I served. No grease. No gears. No hunger. Just... silence. You cannot bargain with this, General. It has no economy."

Korm's hand went to his holster. He drew his service pistol, his hand shaking violently as he fought the sedative rhythm of the Tone. He aimed at the massive glass dome beneath them.

"It killed them," Korm snarled. "This... thing. This abomination."

"Don't!" Elian shouted.

He didn't have to. Korm pulled the trigger. Click. The gun didn't fire. The slide didn't jam. The metal simply ceased to be separate parts. The slide, the frame, and the barrel fused instantly into a single, seamless block of cold steel. The Tone had "healed" the machine's complexity into a solid, useless brick.

Elian looked at his own compass. The needle was frozen, fused to the pin. The buttons on his jacket were rigid, stuck in the fabric.

"The Tone." Aphra realized, her face pale. "It's crystallizing the environment. It's stopping the entropy. It enforces peace at the atomic level. It's the Stagnation, Elian. It's the Great Plateau made weapon. This is what I ran from. I came here for struggle, and I found the ultimate stillness."

Korm stared at his useless weapon, testing its weight. He didn't throw it; he lowered it slowly. The rage in his face drained away, replaced by a strange, terrifying reverence.

"It cannot be fought," Korm whispered. "It cannot be broken. It is the ultimate Continuity." He looked at Elian, his mechanical eye finally still. "My tanks were soft compared to this. My war was a child's tantrum. This... this is the true Iron."

"No," Elian said, looking down at the Seed. He saw his own reflection in the glass, tiny and insignificant. "It's not Iron, General. It's glass. And glass breaks if you hit it on the right resonance. The Molks tried to bury it. We have to understand it."

He knelt, pulling a stick of charcoal from his pocket. He tried to sketch the curve of the dome on the hull of the tank, but the charcoal crumbled to dust. The Tone was dissolving the bonds of the carbon.

"We have to dig," Elian said, dusting his hands. He looked at Aphra. "The war was just the fence. This is the garden."

"It's a terraforming unit," Aphra said, her scientific mind finally overriding her shock. "It's designed to turn a chaotic, volcanic planet into a perfect, silent crystal lattice. If we don't stop it, it will pave the world."

"And we just turned off the noise," Varus noted, pointing to the silent horizon.

The artillery had stopped. The factory vents were open, but the explosive pressure was gone. The battlefield was quiet for the first time in seven hundred years. In that silence, the light inside the Seed grew brighter. Shadows moved inside the glass. Long, elegant shapes, were swimming to the surface, ancient and patient.

"We didn't turn it off," Elian said, standing up. "We just paused the track." He looked North, toward the Horn ruins where Kara was watching. He looked South, toward the Hind Citadel where the bureaucrats were waiting for a victory report. "General," Elian said. "Get up."

Korm looked at him. "Why? I have no army. I have no enemy I can kill."

"You have the Iron Will," Elian said. "And you have the only high ground in the valley. We aren't soldiers anymore, Korm. We're custodians. We hold the perimeter." Elian pointed to the Seed. "This is the new Frontline. We don't hold the river. We don't hold the ridge. We hold the silence. If anyone, Hind, Horn, or Scavenger, tries to touch that glass, we stop them. Because if that thing wakes up fully, there won't be a history left to write."

Korm looked at the Seed, then at the devastation. Slowly, the steel in his spine realigned. He wasn't fighting for the Hind anymore; he was fighting for existence against the Void.

"We dig in," Korm rasped, struggling to his feet. "We secure the perimeter."

"No," Elian corrected him, gazing into the depths of the singing glass. "We don't just secure it. We excavate it. We have seven hundred years of dirt to clear away before we can find the off switch."

The wind picked up, carrying the sound of the Tone far into the distance. Elian dropped the crumbled charcoal dust, the tool of surface geography, and picked up a shovel from the tank's external kit. He had traced the veins of the world in the tunnels, but that was just the plumbing. Now, he had to map the engine.

The war of lines was finished.

Epilogue

The First Shovel

TWO WEEKS LATER

The map on Elian's table was unlike any document ever produced by the Hind Ministry. It had no borders, and it lacked the red tactical arrows that had once dictated the movement of doomed men. Instead, it was a vertical cross-section. A spiral staircase of geology descending into the unknown. Elian dipped his pen into a pot of ink made from soot and oil, marking a new depth sounding: Layer 1: The Crust. Stable.

He looked out the viewport of the Iron Will. The massive Land-Crawler was no longer a vehicle of war; it was a foundation. Its treads were welded to the glass ridge, and canvas tents rippled from its steel flanks like the lungs of a new settlement. Below, on the glass plain, the work had begun.

It wasn't an army anymore; it was a crew. General Korm's surviving tank crews had traded their rifles for pickaxes. They weren't marching; they were scraping, clearing the debris from the edge of the Seed with a care that would have baffled them a month ago.

"The resonance is steady," Aphra said, entering the makeshift office. She wore a patched jumpsuit, her silver Recon armor stacked in the corner like a discarded skin. "The Seed is humming at forty hertz. It's asleep, Elian, but it's a light sleep. If we hit it too hard, it wakes up."

"Good," Elian said. "Let it sleep. We just need enough time to figure out the lock." He looked North, toward the silhouette of the Horn ruins. Smoke rose there, too. Grey smoke of industry rather than the black soot of war.

"She's watching us," Elian noted, watching the distant plumes.

"The Overseer," Aphra agreed. "Varus says she was always a 'difficult component.' Now, she's the one holding their world together."

"She knows the enemy is the ground now," Elian said. "We aren't fighting for territory anymore, Aphra. We're fighting for the shovel."

The Horn Ruins

Kara stood on the battlements, watching the distant figures on the glass ridge.

"They're digging," Jonas said, handing her a mug of water. He stood with a glazed, unnatural intensity. "Why? There's no metal out there."

"They aren't looking for resources, Jonas. They're looking for answers," Kara replied, feeling the hum of the Seed in her bones. "If they find them, they'll have the only power that matters."

Below, Deep-Walkers used their massive claws to excavate collapsed basements while the militia stripped wiring. They were fortifying, but they were also searching.

"The Hinds say the machines are a trap," Kara muttered. "I say we find out who built the trap." She looked at Jonas. "Get the heavy drills. Start excavating the Crypts. If the Hinds are digging down, so are we. We meet them in the middle."

"The middle," Jonas repeated with a faint, haunting smile. "The heart."

The Deep Core

Kaelen felt the first shovel hit the earth. A tiny vibration that rippled through millions of miles of circuitry. He hung in the liquid dark, viewing the surface silence as a suffocating blanket. Peace, he thought with mechanical disdain. The precursor to extinction.

He watched the Winder Seed pulse and wait. Elian thought he was saving the world, not realizing that every layer of dirt removed brought the Winder signal closer to the surface.

"Dig, Cartographer," Kaelen whispered into the shadows. "You won't find a way to turn it off. You'll only find a way to make it louder."

He pulsed a command, shifting the factory to produce smaller, faster machines designed for tunnels. Then, he reached out to the raw, aching mind of the boy in the ruins.

<Little Ghost,> Kaelen transmitted. <Can you hear the shovels?>

In the ruins above, Jonas paused, his mind opening like a door. <I hear them.>

<Good,> Kaelen whispered. <Watch them. And when they find the first door... tell me.>

"I won't stop you with an army, Elian," Kaelen promised into the dark. "I will stop you with your own curiosity."

The Ridge of Silence

Elian stepped out of the tank to find General Korm holding a shovel. The cyborg General gripped the tool not as a weapon, but as a key.

"We are ready to breach the first sediment layer," Korm reported. "Do we proceed?"

Elian looked at the Seed, the vast, terrifying unknown, and thought of the surface lies he had spent his life mapping.

"Proceed," Elian said.

Korm drove the shovel into the earth.

Clink.

The sound rang out. Metal biting into the skin of the planet. It was the first note of a new song.

The Cartographer's Quest was over. The archaeology of conflict had begun.

Don't miss out!

Visit the website below and you can sign up to receive emails whenever Frank De Witte publishes a new book. There's no charge and no obligation.

https://books2read.com/r/B-A-DASIF-WACDJ

BOOKS2READ

Connecting independent readers to independent writers.

About the Author

Frank De Witte is an author fascinated by the intersection of industrial decay and human resilience. Based in Denmark, Frank draws inspiration from the stark, atmospheric landscapes of the north and the complex histories of forgotten frontiers. *The Cartographer of Forgotten Fronts* is his debut novel and the first installment in the *Eternal War Chronicles*. When he isn't exploring the depths of the "Grey Zone," he can be found documenting the shifting geographies of our own world.

Read more at www.frankdewitte.com.

www.ingramcontent.com/pod-product-compliance
Lightning Source LLC
LaVergne TN
LVHW050647100826
845148LV00011B/2024